THE TREEHOUSE

ANDREW J BRANDT

CAPROCK PUBLISHING GROUP
AMARILLO

Copyright © 2019 Andrew J Brandt

This is a work of fiction. Names, characters, businesses, places, events, locales, and incidents are either the products of the author's imagination or used in a fictitious manner. Any resemblance to actual persons, living or dead, or actual events is purely coincidental.

Originally published April 2019 independently.

Cover Design: Caprock Concepts

ISBN: 9781077426115

DEDICATION

To Jennifer, for believing in me from the very beginning.

To my kids for the inspiration for this story. Stay out of trouble, kiddos.

CONTENTS

ACKNOWLEDGMENTS

Although I've been writing for years—a dozen stop-start stories reside on my laptop—*The Treehouse* was the first one to come out intact. Like digging a dinosaur, sometimes you only find fragments. I was lucky that this one came out whole. I had a lot of help and inspiration along the way. Kenny Nagunst and 806 Sports, thank you for the radio air time to allow me to share my passion. Anthony Pittman and Nicole Caan at ABC 7, thank you for the encouragement. And everyone who bought the book, thank you for making a guy's dream come true.

-Andrew

FACT:

In a survey of 110 junior and senior high school students in Texas, 55 admitted to sneaking out at least once.

FACT:

170 children go missing in Texas every year.

ANDREW J BRANDT

PART ONE
THE BODY IN THE WOODS

ANDREW J BRANDT

CHAPTER 1
FRIDAY 14 MARCH | 10:55PM

"OW! SHIT!" THE words left the eleven-year-old boy's mouth almost instinctively. He'd never cursed before, but the hammer hitting his thumb – instead of the nail he was holding – made the word come out effortlessly. Lucas dropped the hammer and shook his hand. The hammer thudded against the wooden planks that made up the floor of the treehouse. His thumb throbbed and pulsed, and he stuck it in his mouth.

The two other boys in the treehouse tried to contain their laughter as Lucas held his thumb in his mouth, but to little avail.

"I'm gonna tell your dad you said 'shit'," Tyler said, giggling almost uncontrollably at the last word.

"Yeah, you shouldn't say 'shit', Lucas," the third boy, Elijah said.

"Shut up, guys! It really hurts!" Lucas held out his hand to show his friends where he'd hit it. The thumb was red and showed the beginnings of a bruise, but there was no blood and he moved the thumb back and forth to ensure he hadn't broken the digit.

Lucas had been hammering up an Avengers poster on the wall of the treehouse—the fort, they called it—when the mishap occurred. The three boys committed to spend the night in their new hangout in the woods once the project was complete. After some round-robin explanations to their parents of where they would be that evening, they couldn't think of anything more perfect than spending the first night of their first middle school spring break in their new fort.

The woods just beyond their neighborhood was full of these large pine trees that could reach over a hundred feet high with bases anywhere between four to six feet in diameter—perfect for supporting a treehouse.

The fort itself was a project the boys had been working on since Christmas break. Though they were often told to not venture too far out into the woods, the three boys would spend countless hours after school playing and exploring. Once the idea of a treehouse came up, they searched for a perfect tree as their base. Using any extra money they had to purchase supplies, as well as scrounging up any scrap lumber they could find (including, fortuitously enough, stealing the leftover scrap wood from a home renovation that had occurred in their neighborhood over the course of the fall), the three of them would haul their materials by hand the few hundred yards out into the woods. Lucas begged his sister Allison, who had a car, to take him to the hardware store to buy screws and nails. Her demand? Thirty dollars for the ride and to keep the whole thing a secret from their parents.

The plans and design for the treehouse came from a copy of *The Dangerous Book for Boys* that Elijah's grandmother had given him as a Christmas present. Following the instructions in the book, they were able to screw in two long four-by-four studs into the base of the tree at about five feet above the ground. From that base, the boys laid down eight-foot-long two-by-fours as the floor foundation, with the tree trunk piercing through the middle of the frame. Once that was finished, they created walls using two-by-fours and scraps of plywood. The roof was completed by screwing more two-by-fours higher up on the tree base and draping more plywood over them, nailing the sheets to the planks. Finally, after nearly three months of working on it, the fort was finally "done." To the three friends it was perfect and, for a while, they simply stared at it. The treehouse was this marvel, this thing they'd made with their own hands. It was a place of their own, away from parents and school and bullies. It was their own oasis in the woods.

For their first night in the treehouse, each boy brought snacks, a sleeping bag and a few personal items they thought would make the place "really freaking cool"—Tyler's current catchphrase.

"Did one of you guys bring the drinks?" Lucas asked, the pain in his thumb subsiding.

Tyler reached into his backpack, pulled out three bottles of Mountain Dew and tossed them to his friends. They all sat around the floor of their treehouse and twisted open the sodas.

"My mom doesn't let me have these at home," Elijah said between gulps. "I don't know why though! Sometimes I think my parents just don't want me to have any fun. Like, what's the difference between this and regular Coke?"

Tyler took a long sip from his bottle. "I know what you mean. Parents suck sometimes."

"For sure. My mom said I have to be back home by ten thirty in the morning because she has to work tomorrow. I have to spend my whole Saturday watching my sister!" Elijah rolled his eyes and tipped his bottle back for another swig.

Lucas looked around the treehouse, examining their handiwork. "I can't believe we finally finished this place. We can keep whatever we want out here and our parents will never have to know," said Lucas. "I have a few more things to bring this week. We need more lights and something to listen to music with."

"My dad has a really freaking cool Bluetooth speaker in the garage he doesn't use. I bet I can get it," Tyler said, continuing to drink his soda.

"That would be awesome!" Elijah nearly burped the last word and all three boys laughed.

"You know what else is awesome? I can't believe sixth grade is almost over," Lucas said. "Do you guys know what classes you're gonna take next year?"

"I don't know," said Tyler. "My dad really wants me to play basketball. He said he was a point guard and that I'm built like him. But I just don't know if I want to play sports."

"Yeah, my mom doesn't want me to play football. She said I could do any other sport." Elijah took another gulp from his Mountain Dew, finishing the bottle off. "I may sign up for soccer, but I haven't played since we were in the fourth grade."

"I remember that!" quipped Lucas. "You were so fast! I would throw the ball in really far down the field because I knew you would beat everyone else to it."

"Too bad I sucked at actually kicking the ball!"

All three laughed at that.

Elijah continued, "Maybe I'll sign up for track. I just don't want to do a whole lot of running."

Lucas laughed, "That's all track is, dude!"

"Hey Lucas, does your sister still have her boyfriend?" Tyler asked.

"Yes, and she said she will never go out with you so quit asking."

Tyler rolled his eyes to Lucas's reply. "She thinks she's too good for me, it's all good. Just wait til I'm in high school. She won't be able to resist me. I'll be the coolest dude at Henderson High."

"Except she'll be, like, twenty when we're in high school!"

As Lucas and Tyler bantered back and forth about Lucas's older sister, Elijah opened up his backpack and pulled out an LED lantern. "I found this in my closet last weekend. Figured we'd need it up here for at night."

"I wish we had something to make a fire so we could have s'mores," said Lucas. "But a fire in a tree would probably not be a good thing." They all laughed at the idea of a campfire in the middle of their treehouse. "Just think! We wouldn't have to go get firewood!"

As they continued their banter, the back and forth and talking about life, school and girls, Lucas took delight in the treehouse and the fact that they were able to get it to the point that they were spending the night in it. Spring break in East Texas was usually very calm and cool, but not too cold. The temperature could get down in the low-fifties at night, but the boys figured with enough blankets and the walls of the treehouse keeping the air out that they'd be fine. The four walls were made up of particle boards supported by two-by-fours, with a single window cut out of one of the panels, so there weren't too many holes for the wind to come through.

Lucas noticed that Tyler's voice was already changing, getting deeper. His and Elijah's were still high-pitched, not having reached puberty yet. He often wondered when that would happen. And what would happen? And how? Would he wake up one day with hair under his armpits and an Adam's apple? He wanted to ask Tyler, but he was also embarrassed.

He pulled his phone out of his backpack to check the time. It was just after one in the morning, but he was nowhere near feeling tired. The excitement of being in the treehouse—and probably coupled with the caffeine from the sodas—was keeping sleep at bay, at least for now.

"Are you guys hungry? I brought some peanut butter and jellies," Lucas said.

His friends gladly took the sandwiches that he pulled from his bag and though they were slightly smashed from being tossed in there with the rest of his stuff, they were protected in sandwich bags.

"Seriously guys, maybe we can make a fire pit outside and we can make hot dogs or something," Lucas said as he bit into his own sandwich. "My dad makes these things called 'hobo dinners' when we go camping and they're super easy. It's just chicken and vegetables and you wrap it all in foil and cook it right in the campfire."

"I can't wait for summer," said Elijah. "We can spend every single day out here."

"Is your mom going to make you babysit your sister this summer?" Lucas asked. Elijah's mom and dad separated and his dad moved to Austin just before Thanksgiving.

"I don't think so. I hope not. I'm too young to take care of a five-year-old! It's not my fault she and my dad couldn't get along. So, I shouldn't be punished. She's not going to ruin my summer."

"My dad wants me to go to this basketball camp at SFU this summer. But it's only like two weeks," Tyler said. He finished his sandwich, pushing the last bite into his mouth. "He thinks I'm just like him. It's like he wants me to do everything he did."

"Would you have to stay in Nacogdoches?" Lucas asked.

"Yeah, it's like this whole camp thing. Something to prepare for, like, competitive basketball. He says colleges are going to start looking at me in a couple of years."

"Well, just don't forget about us when you're up there with Steph Curry!" said Elijah.

"Man, I'm never gonna be as good as—" Tyler cut himself off and cocked his head. "Do you guys hear that?"

The other two boys both silenced themselves and listened. Tyler lowered his voice and whispered, "I heard someone out there. Turn off the light."

When building the treehouse, the boys used a piece of plywood and some blocks to hold it in place over the window cutout. Elijah turned out the LED lantern and Tyler slowly removed the plywood window.

The first thing Lucas thought was that they'd been caught. Someone's mom called someone else's and they'd been found out. Or, his sister Allison ratted him out to their parents. His heart pounded in his chest, knowing that they'd look out the window and see all of their parents coming out to the woods—this secret place, their hideout.

The moonlight illuminated just enough of the area that he could see that there were no parents outside, no flashlight beams coming their way. Lucas breathed a sigh of relief but choked up again when he heard a sound.

A grunt, or a cough, in these woods travelled far. The boys couldn't see anything, but they darted their eyes about, trying to make out the source of the sound. Again, a grunt. The shuffling of feet in dirt and leaves.

There, just a few yards out the window, Lucas saw it. He pointed so his friends could see what he was seeing. It was a man trudging, laboriously, through the woods. He was carrying something large draped across his shoulders. From the rustling sound, it seemed to be a trash bag—a large trash bag with something heavy inside.

Lucas's heart beat even faster than before, though his body felt paralyzed. He didn't know what was going on. Could the man see them as well, up in the tree? Could he hear them?

The man dropped whatever he was carrying on his shoulders onto the ground in front of a fallen tree log. He had a shovel in one hand, and he started to dig. The three boys watched for—what felt like to them—an eternity as this man dug a hole in the soft earth.

Finally, the man shoved the trash bag and its contents into the hole, covered it up with dirt and leaves and attempted to roll the fallen log over his handiwork. Once he was done he ran off, back toward the city, out of the woods.

The three boys slumped down onto the floor of their treehouse. Lucas felt sweat on his palms and on his forehead. He looked at Tyler, his eyes large and full of fear. Elijah was holding his legs up against his chest.

Neither of them said a word.

Tyler slowly reached up and slid the window back into place over the framed hole.

"Guys, what did we just see? What was that?" Elijah's voice cracked, breaking the silence and darkness. It was the first sound any of them had made in almost an hour.

Tyler looked at Lucas and Elijah, the same fear still in his eyes. He said, "That was a body."

ANDREW J BRANDT

CHAPTER TWO
SATURDAY MARCH 15 | 12:45AM

ALLISON HANES CHECKED the time. It was almost one in the morning, and she'd been gone for nearly an hour at this point. She knew she was risking it being out at this time, but she figured that her parents had gone to bed at around ten and her brother was spending the night with one of his little friends.

The Dodge Challenger's windows were fogged over with breath and body heat. Her boyfriend put his shirt back on and handed the girl hers. She clasped her bra back together and pulled the black American Eagle t-shirt over her head, pulling her long brown hair through the hole. She had light brown hair that fell nearly to the small of her back.

The keys to the Dodge Challenger were in the ignition and turned backward so the radio played while the

17

two teenagers made out. A song by Marianas Trench played on the speakers from the girl's iPhone plugged into the aux.

"We need to find a better place than this. I don't like the park," Allison said. "It's too busy. Someone is going to see your car here." Yates Park was a popular place in the spring and summer for little league soccer and pickup softball games. At night, however, the park was empty and quiet. City ordinance in Henderson stated that no one was allowed in the park after 11:00pm though that didn't stop teenagers from using it as a frequent hookup destination.

"I don't think anyone that lives on this side of town knows me enough to know this is my car," the young man said.

Kilgore Drive, the main strip that ran through town, was the separator between the have's and have-not's in Henderson. Yates Park was on the have-not side.

"Brandon. Everyone knows this car."

Allison also hated making out in the backseat of a Dodge Challenger. She'd rather be with her boyfriend in the comfort of her bedroom or even in the roomier backseat of her Jeep Liberty, but that couldn't be an option tonight. There was no way she could get her vehicle out of the driveway without her parents noticing. And technically, her parents forbid her from having a boyfriend.

"How about next time you park up the street from my house and come to my window?" she asked

Brandon pulled the visor mirror down to check his hair. It was sticking in every direction. Allison had run her fingers all through it, giving it a light tug during their making out. "Yeah, I could do that. I just don't want my car sitting in front of some rando's house in the middle of the night. Maybe your parents could, like, chill, for a minute and you wouldn't have to sneak around with me. I'm a nice guy. They'd like me."

"They don't like anyone. I can just hear my mom now—I warned you about boys like that."

Brandon shook his head at that. "She'd like me. I'd make her like me. She wouldn't have a choice. I'd tell her all about going to church and stuff."

"She may buy it, but my stepdad would see right through your bullshit, Brandon." And she was right. Her dad was very much a no-nonsense kind of guy, and one look at this jock with his muscle car and Mr. Bobby Beaker would shut the door directly in the kid's face.

Allison just hated having to sneak around with Brandon though. She enjoyed being with him, and he made her feel pretty. Every time she went back home to pretend he wasn't a part of her life, though, she felt empty. She just wanted these last two years of high school to be over so she could do whatever she wanted. She even thought about going to college in

Lubbock, or even further away, just so she could feel like she had some freedom for once. Yet, she dreaded the idea of being away from him.

Allison watched Brandon fix his hair in the mirror and make sure he wiped off all her lip gloss from his lips and neck. This big, stupid boy, she thought. The love of her life, if she were allowed to have a life. His shaggy walnut hair and big blue eyes and chiseled face. He was so handsome. Two of his best friends went down to Austin for spring break, but he stayed here, which she was glad for. She couldn't stand the idea of going a whole week without spending time with him.

"So maybe tomorrow night you can come through the window," she said, almost a question.

"Yeah, babe. I'll see what I can do. I've got baseball drills in the morning and then I've gotta help my dad at the store, but I can make time for you tomorrow night."

"Hey, have you thought about where you're going next year?" she asked.

"Yeah," he said. "I'm gonna stay at SFU. They offered me that good baseball scholarship, so I'm going to take it. It means I can stay close to you. Then maybe you can come after next year?"

Stephen F. Austin University, located in Nacogdoches, was just an hour's drive away from their small town of Henderson. Allison knew she could handle that. He could come home on the weekends when he wasn't playing, and she'd be able to drive to Nacogdoches to watch him play.

"I'd like that, a lot." Even though SFU wasn't her first choice, Allison knew she was willing to make the sacrifice to stay with Brandon. She really wanted to go to Baylor or Texas A&M. Her best friend Amilyn got accepted to A&M next year. The thought that she'd be all alone hit her all of a sudden. Her boyfriend and best friend would both be off to college while she had to stay for one more year before her own graduation.

She supposed Brandon could see the sadness in her eyes. "Are you sure?" he asked her. "Doesn't look like you like it very much."

"I do, I'm just worried about next year since you'll be gone."

"Don't worry, babe. I'll be back in town as often as possible." He smiled at her and kissed her on the nose.

Brandon's reassurance didn't sit well in her stomach, but she smiled nonetheless. "I should be getting home soon. I don't want to be gone too long."

Brandon reached for the ignition, but something stopped him from turning the key. A puzzled look flashed across his face and he cocked his ear. "Did you hear that?" he asked Allison.

"Did I hear what?" Allison tried to listen. She ran the palm of her hand over the fogged windshield to clear a section of the glass so that she could see through. She hoped they hadn't been found by the police, and she hoped doubly that it wasn't Tyler Washington's father. Just as their sons, Tyler and Lucas, John Washington and Bobby were close friends, and it wouldn't take long for Mr. Washington to tell her stepdad about this secret midnight rendezvous at Yates Park. She'd be grounded for the rest of the school year, she was sure. Allison squinted her eyes to adjust to the dark and saw movement across the street from the park.

"Babe, look!" she said, pointing

Brandon rapidly cleared a spot in the windshield for himself and peered out.

There, across the street from the park, was a row of such houses. The paneling on several was chipped and dilapidated. A car sat in front of one of the homes, an older black Ford sedan. Somehow it looked to not belong in the neighborhood to Allison. Something seemed...off. She quickly realized that the black Ford was running, but its lights were dark. And the trunk was open.

The source of the sound wasn't necessarily coming from the car, however. Both Allison and Brandon looked on in horror as they watched a person, a man, load a large package in the opened trunk of the Ford. Despite the darkness, it was apparent to Allison that the package was a body wrapped in a black trash bag.

The man then shut the trunk lid quietly, opened the driver's door, got in the car and drove away. The two teenagers watched as his tail lights faded off for a few blocks toward the south end of town.

"Oh my god, Brandon. What just happened?" Allison asked in a hyperventilated whisper. "Was that a body?!" Her voice cut the quiet between them and all awareness rushed back into Brandon's brain.

"I don't know babe. Just calm down."

"Calm down?! Brandon, that guy just loaded a body in the back of that car!" Her voice was loud now, terror raising it to a near scream.

Brandon took the girl's hand in his own. She was trembling profusely. Her breath out of rhythm and heavy as he stroked her fingers in an attempt to get her to relax. "We don't know that," he said in a half-attempt to reassure her. "But we need to get out of here. If someone else saw, that means the cops will be here soon."

"Are you sure he's gone?" Allison wiped her hands on the rest of the fogged windows to remove the condensation. Peering out through the windshield and the door window, she didn't notice anyone else roused in the neighborhood or around the park, at least not anyone who would be immediately apparent.

"Yeah babe, I think he's gone. C'mon, let's get out

of here," Brandon said.

Brandon turned the ignition, the matte black Challenger roaring to life. Allison's house was only a few blocks away across Kilgore Drive, but she sat in complete silence the entire ride. Her almond eyes framed in long lashes, the mascara all rubbed off, stared at the porch lights of the houses as they drove past. Brandon held her hand as he drove, occasionally releasing it to shift gears.

When they arrived to her neighborhood, Brandon parked across the street and two houses down. Allison gave Brandon a quick kiss on the lips. "I'll see you tomorrow," she said.

She got of the car and hurriedly jogged back to her house. All she wanted to do was crawl back through her window, wrap up under her bedsheets and forget this night happened.

CHAPTER THREE
SATURDAY MARCH 15 | 1:54AM

THE BOYS IN the treehouse sat in the darkness, afraid to turn the LED lantern back on. There wasn't a sound in the woods, no more rustling of leaves or of shoes on the dirt. Lucas could still hear the sound of the man's shovel stabbing into the earth in his mind's ear. He couldn't stop thinking about what he and his friends had just witnessed, however none of them could bring themselves to speak.

Finally, Tyler broke the silence with a whisper, "I think we're okay now, guys. I haven't heard anything in almost," he illuminated the hands on his Timex watch, "fifteen minutes."

Elijah spoke up as well, his voice cracking, prepubescent and fearful, "I want to go home, guys."

Lucas did as well, but he didn't know what to do.

He knew that he couldn't tell his parents about the hideout, in fear of their reaction to their secret. They'd make him and his friends tear it down. He may even not be allowed to hang out with them anymore. "I think we should get our stuff and get out of here," he said.

Elijah said, "Yeah, let's pack up. We can go to my house. We can go through the backdoor through the garage. My mom should be asleep, and she won't hear us if we're quiet."

Tyler nodded in agreement, grabbing his backpack. "We can't have any evidence that we were out here. Our parents will kill us."

"Don't say that, man," Lucas said. "Somebody really is dead out there!"

"You know what I mean!" Tyler said. "No one can know this is our treehouse. The cops will probably be out here in the morning and will want to question anyone who saw what we saw. And I don't know about you guys, but I know for a fact my parents will ground me for forever if they knew we were out here."

Tyler reached for the lantern. Turning the LED light back on, the treehouse suddenly bathed in a light glow. All three boys quickly packed up everything they could that looked like personal property into their backpacks. All the trash from their sodas, candy and other food they threw into a grocery store plastic sack and Elijah chucked it into his blue Champion backpack.

Lucas looked at the Avengers poster, sighed and ripped it from the nails he'd hammered in earlier in the night. He rolled the poster up and shoved it into his own backpack. He took account of all his belongings, his phone, external battery pack and asthma inhaler.

The boys gave the treehouse one last look-over to make sure they got it all. "It has to look like no one has been here recently," Tyler said. Lucas thought they did a good job of clearing everything out. The floor and walls were completely empty. At one time, Lucas thought it would be cool to paint the interior of the fort, but for now it was brown, bare wood.

Elijah opened the trap door and peered out to the ground below. No boogeyman waited for them at the base of the tree. "Okay guys, let's go," he said. He looked at the rope ladder they'd built to get in and out but decided to leave it coiled to the side. "We can jump down."

First Elijah and then Lucas shimmied through the trapdoor on the floor and jumped to the ground. Tyler went last, throwing down the backpacks to his friends before jumping down himself. Lucas handed Tyler's backpack to him when he reached the ground and he swung it over his shoulders.

The three boys trekked back through the trees, refraining from using the lantern in fear of being noticed, for several hundred yards until they reached the long fence line of their neighborhood that separated the houses and yards from the woods. Elijah's house was just on the next street beyond the houses that butted up against the trees.

Sweat dripped down Lucas's forehead and he didn't know if it was from the strenuous walk for from the stress and anxiety he was feeling in his gut. Nonetheless it felt cold with the nighttime air hitting his face. The boys crossed the block to the street where Elijah lived, watching for any cars or other activity in the area. The neighborhood was quiet and black. There were cars parked out in front of some houses, but everything was dark and lifeless.

They reached their destination, going through the alley to Elijah's backyard. Climbing as quietly as possible over the chain link fence that separated yard from alley, they helped toss bags and backpacks until each of them made it over the barrier. Elijah pulled out a key hanging from a chain around his neck and unlocked the door that led into the garage from the backyard. Lucas, the last one in, shut it as slowly as he could in order to not make any sound. The door creaked, but he didn't think it was loud enough for Elijah's mother to hear if she were asleep. Once they were in the garage, Elijah did the same with the door leading into the house.

The door opened up into a utility room, with a washer and dryer, and the kitchen was just beyond through a doorless entrance. A light above the kitchen sink illuminated the kitchen, the white appliances illuminated from the it. The light, and the house itself, made Lucas feel safe. He noticed his breathing, which had been heavy and hurried, had calmed down to normal.

The three boys entered Elijah's bedroom and deposited their backpacks on the floor. "My mom has to work in the morning. We'll tell her we came back here to play Xbox. I don't think she'll mind if you guys stay for a little while," Elijah said in a half-whisper.

He didn't think his mom was awake, and he'd certainly not want to disturb her now. He sat on the edge of his bed, a messy full-sized unit with a blue comforter and sheets crumpled at the foot. A basket of clothes overflowing was at the foot of the bed. Elijah pulled his shoes off and tossed them beside the clothes basket.

"My parents already think I'm here," Tyler said, removing his shoes as well.

"Yeah, and I'll just text my dad in the morning. I'll tell him I came over here with Tyler," said Lucas.

Lucas sat on a blue bean bag chair on the ground, its faux-leather surface cracked with age and wear. Tyler was in the chair at the computer desk, his feet stretched out in front of him.

"Well, this is definitely not how I thought our first night in the fort would go," Elijah said. He fell backward onto the mattress, his head hitting a Spider-man pillow. "I wonder if we'll ever get to go back."

"We'll get to go back," Tyler said. "Once the cops get everything figured out. It'll probably be a couple of days but think about this. It's just like a movie; someone goes missing, right? So, they're gonna do a search party, and they'll have, like, body-sniffing dogs. So, they'll find the body, catch the bad guy, and things will go back to normal."

"You're right," Lucas said, reclining back onto the beanbag. "We've just got to stay quiet for a few days and it'll all be back to normal." Lucas's words ended with a yawn. Now that they were in a house, away from the woods and safe, exhaustion started weighing on his eyelids.

As he closed his eyes, Lucas couldn't get the sound the shovel out of his head. The sound it made as it tore into the ground, slicing the dirt, looped in his mind. And the way the bag that the body was in sounded as it hit the bottom of the newly-dug hole. The heavy thud. He shook it out of his mind. He wanted to forget it, hoping that in the morning, things would begin to go back to normal.

As he fell asleep, he chanted in his head silently like a mantra, *Things will go back to normal.*

CHAPTER FOUR
SATURDAY MARCH 15 | 10:34AM

A PUDDLE OF drool formed in the corner of Lucas's mouth and he wiped it off as he rustled awake. His blonde hair was disheveled, with one chunk matted to the side of his face while in the back a cowlick stood straight up. He slept hard and dreamless on the beanbag chair. He sat up to see Elijah still soundly asleep on his bed. Tyler was on the floor with his pillow and sleeping bag that he had brought from the treehouse as his bedding.

Reaching for his backpack, Lucas pulled his phone out to check the time. The iPhone 5—a hand-me-down from his older sister—read 10:35am. He had no missed texts from his parents, which was good. He unlocked the device and opened the messaging app. He thumbed out a quick text to his dad. *Good morning dad.*

I'm at Elijah's with Elijah and Tyler. Just wanted to let you know. He made sure the ringer was on and put the device back in his bag.

There was a knock at the bedroom door. "Elijah, mijo, are you home?" Elijah's mom opened the door. As it opened, she fumbled with her long dark hair, wrapping it in a ponytail. "Oh, goodness," she said, startled to see all three boys in there, "I didn't know you boys were here!"

Elijah sat up on his bed and rubbed his eyes, "Sorry, mom. Yeah. We came in last night. We wanted to play Fortnite on the Xbox. I didn't want to wake you up when we came in, so we tried to stay quiet."

Tyler also woke up, stretching and yawning. "Hi, Ms. Reyes," Tyler said. "I hope you don't mind us being here."

"Oh, not at all," she said. She pulled her car keys from the front pocket of her nurse's scrubs and gave her attention to Elijah. "I have to go to work, mijo. There's stuff for lunch in the fridge. Make sure your sister brushes her teeth. I'll be home at seven. I love you."

"I love you, mom," Elijah said. "Is it okay if Lucas and Tyler stay over for a little while? We're going to have a Fortnite tournament."

She smiled, "Yes, as long as you stay here with your sister, I don't mind." With that, she shut the door and left. Lucas ran his hands through his hair, trying to tame the wildness. His mouth felt dry and he reached into his backpack where he still had a bottle of water. Lucas twisted the cap off the Ozarka bottle and took an excessive gulp. The room temperature water felt good on his dry throat.

"Can I have a drink of that?" Tyler asked. Lucas handed it over to his friend. Tyler also took a large swig from the bottle. "Man," Tyler said, shaking his head and blinking his eyes, forcing himself fully awake. "I don't know about you guys, but I slept like a rock."

Both Lucas and Elijah agreed. Once the adrenaline rush ran its course, coupled with the late-night hike back through the woods and the neighborhood, sleep came easy and heavy. However, the events of the night were still fresh in their minds and imaginations.

"What are we going to do now, guys?" Lucas asked. "I mean, are we really just going to wait around and hope the police or somebody finds that body?"

"Here's what I think," Tyler said, sitting up and sliding out of his sleeping bag on the floor. "We can stay quiet for a little while. Besides, we don't actually know that it was a body. It could have been something else. Maybe a dead dog or—"

Elijah cut him off, "I don't know, man. That would have been a really big dog."

Lucas nodded his head, "Yeah, who buries a dog in

the middle of the night, and in the woods?"

"What I'm saying is," said Tyler, "we don't one hundred percent know. So, I say we stay quiet for a little while. I don't want any of us to get in trouble or get grounded. But, if we hear something about a missing person, we can always call the cops but not tell them who we are. My dad says he gets anonymous tips all the time about stuff."

Lucas nodded in agreement. "You're right. We can watch the news, see if there's anything on Facebook about somebody missing. If there is, we make a call to the cops."

"Did either of you guys see what he looked like?" asked Elijah.

Lucas shook his head. "Not really well. I could tell that he was big though." Lucas kept playing the whole ordeal in his head, racking his brain for any other details. All he could remember, however, was the dark shape of a man digging that hole by the fallen tree trunk. The way the man worked quickly and methodically.

"I couldn't take my eyes off him," Tyler said. "He was built like a football player. He was wearing a hoodie though so I couldn't really see his face. But he was definitely a big guy. Almost as big as your dad," he nodded to Elijah.

"I wish we would have built that treehouse some-where else," Elijah said, his head hanging low. Lucas knew the reference to Elijah's father, whom he hadn't seen since Christmas, made his friend sad.

"I'm going to check the internet, see if there's any-thing about a missing person," Lucas said, taking the attention away from the subject of Elijah's father. He pulled his phone out of his backpack. There was a mes-sage notification from his dad. *Sounds good. Will you be home for lunch?* He pecked out a quick reply. *No. Probably around 2:00. Playing Fortnite.*

"What's the newspaper called?" he asked his friends. None of them had ever actually read a news-paper. To them, it was something only adults did, and usually only when they were looking for information about garage sales.

"I think it's just called The Henderson News," Eli-jah said.

Lucas googled "henderson tx news" and the news-paper's website was the first result. He clicked through to the website to see the first news report: "Local teen reported missing."

"Guys! Look at this!" he exclaimed. He couldn't be-lieve his eyes. His friends crowded on either shoulder to see his phone screen.

He clicked through to the story, which was just a small blurb. "Officials are searching for local teen girl reported missing early Saturday morning. Details will come as they are made available. If you see this girl, please contact the police. She is described as Hispanic with black hair and brown eyes, 5-foot-2 and 90lbs." There was a picture of the girl with her name underneath, Ariel Perez.

"This is it!" Lucas said. "We have to go to the cops!"

"Okay," said Tyler. "Let's do this: let's go back out to the fort. Let's make sure we didn't leave anything. Then we can come back and make the call. I think there's a payphone in front of the 7-11 over off Kilgore Drive we can call from. We can't use our cell phones because the cops can trace that."

Lucas liked the plan. They'd be able to protect themselves and at the same time help the police find the body and solve the case. It made him feel good to know that they potentially had the information that could solve a real crime. He thought about the Avengers poster in the treehouse and how the superheroes would act in this situation.

"You guys will have to go without me," Elijah said. "I don't think I left anything out there, but if I did, please get it."

"You got it," Lucas said. He grabbed his backpack and turned to Tyler, "Let's get our bikes. I'll run home to get mine and meet you at your house." He was ready to be a superhero.

* * *

Twenty minutes later, Lucas rolled into Tyler's driveway on his blue Huffy. Tyler was sitting on the front porch, waiting for his friend. His bicycle, a red Mongoose, rested on its kickstand. "You ready to do this?" Lucas asked.

"Yeah I am. The sooner we do this, the sooner things will go back to normal. Who would have thought this is how we'd spend our spring break?" Tyler pulled his own backpack onto his shoulders and kicked the kickstand.

"No way," Lucas said, pedaling to ride next to Tyler. "But we get the chance to do something really big. If we help solve this case, and it's the missing girl out there in the woods, that makes us, like, heroes!"

The blue sky above the boys was cloudless and the sunlight was warm. To Lucas, it felt very different from the night before. Last night he was cold and scared. But today? Today was different. He pedaled with an intensity and drive, that he was meant to do something right.

They reached the edge of the woods and parked their bikes next to a tree. So far there was no police presence nearby. Lucas assumed that if the body had already been found, there would have been crime scene tape blocking off access to this part of the woods. Instead, it was just as quiet and empty as any other normal day.

They hiked through the trees, wary of any poison ivy, though the two boys had the path to the treehouse mapped out in their mind, having made this exact walk dozens of times over the last few months.

"Should we check the hole that guy dug?" Lucas asked, stepping over a small stump.

Tyler shook his head. "No way, man. I don't want to even look at it. It gives me the creeps."

"That guy must have had tunnel vision because he wasn't very far away. Maybe from us to," Lucas looked around and pointed at a large dead pine, its branches naked of any leaves, "that dead tree over there?"

"Yeah, he was close enough for me to tell what he was wearing. I just wish I had gotten a better look at him. It would be nice to be able to give the cops some actual details."

The boys were getting close to their destination when they turned around a bend in their trail and saw the treehouse.

Or, more appropriately, they saw the treehouse's remains. Their work, everything they had committed their time to over the course of three months, lay in shambles on the forest floor. The base of the fort was intact, the bottom support studs screwed into the pine tree trunk. However, the walls and roof were completely destroyed. Some were broken in two, like the whole thing had been hit with a wrecking ball. Panels of plywood and wood studs were strewn all around the tree's trunk.

Lucas's eyes widened and filled with tears. He blinked, hoping his eyes were playing tricks on him. He wanted to cry. Every hour, every dollar, every day working on this fort, lay in a heap in front of him.

Tyler grabbed Lucas by the shirt while simultaneously backpedaling. Lucas looked at his friend, and saw his pupils dilate with fear. "Lucas. *Run!*"

ANDREW J BRANDT

CHAPTER FIVE
SATURDAY MARCH 15 | 9:19AM

ALLISON TOSSED AND turned all night, sleep evading her at every tick of the hour. She put her Airpods in and tried listening to a podcast, hoping it would help ease her mind and take her thoughts off what she had witnessed at the park. It didn't work however as every time she closed her eyes, she saw the dark figure dumping the trash bag in the trunk of the car.

She desperately wanted to talk to someone about it, but who? If her parents were to find out that she was sneaking out at night—much less sneaking out with her secret boyfriend—she'd be in more trouble than she could even imagine. The last thing she wanted was to finish her junior year being grounded. She even worried that her parents wouldn't allow her to go to prom next month if they were to find out about her nighttime

43

activities.

She looked at her phone to check the time. It wasn't even ten. She couldn't remember the last time she had woken up before ten on a Saturday. She checked her Instagram and Snapchats. As she scrolled through, pictures of her friends enjoying themselves in other places made her jealous. Amilyn was in San Antonio; there were nearly a dozen selfies of her in front of the Riverwalk. Eating tacos, feeding ducks, taking a boat ride—each picture immaculately framed and edited. Another friend was in Phoenix watching spring training baseball. Another was on a cruise with her family. All these pictures of better lives, just taunting her.

She put the phone on her bedside charging station and decided to get out of bed. The smell of coffee emanated down the long hallway from the kitchen, which meant at least one of her parents was awake. She figured some company and conversation of some kind would help ease her mind.

Pulling on a pair of Nike sweatpants from her floor and straightening her bra under the shirt she'd worn the night before, she walked out of her room. She noticed Lucas's door was open, but he wasn't there. If she remembered correctly, he was spending the night with his friend Tyler—whom she couldn't stand, for the record. Little boys could be so obnoxious sometimes.

The hallway of their home opened up into the living

room and kitchen. Her stepdad, in an old college T-shirt and black sweatpants, was sitting at the breakfast bar that separated the kitchen from the living room. He had a cup of coffee in front of him and reading something on his iPad.

"Hey Alley-cat," he said. He had called her that from nearly the first time she met him. Allison's biological father had left when she was still a baby, and her mother had met Bobby only a year later. She had no memories as a child of any other 'dad' than Bobby. She couldn't bring herself to call him dad, though. She didn't even know why; it was like there was something mentally blocking her from calling him that. "You're up early."

"Yeah, I guess so." She reached up into a cupboard above the sink and pulled out a coffee mug that had a random insurance agency logo on it. She poured herself a cup and topped it off with French vanilla creamer from a carton sitting out on the counter.

"You know, I've been drinking coffee for a long time, and it finally hit me—I don't really like coffee. I just like creamer," Bobby said. This made her smile.

"I guess that means Starbucks has made a killing off of people like you then," she said. She took a seat on an empty barstool at the end of the bar. A plate stacked with blueberry muffins still warm from the oven rested on the bar top. Allison took one and spread a knob of butter from the accompanying dish.

"That's how business works." He took a long sip from his mug. "Find a market and capitalize."

Bobby was a construction project estimator, which meant he was a numbers guy more than anything. There were many weekend mornings where he could be found sitting in this exact spot with his mug of coffee, going over numbers and budgets or even reading project manuals on his iPad.

"Is mom still in bed?" Allison asked.

"No, she left this morning to go show a house to a new couple moving to town," Bobby replied.

Allison started thinking again about the night before. Who would want to move here? This is where people are shoved into trunks in trash bags.

Bobby noticed out of the corner of his eye his daughter sitting there, sullen and silent. "You okay?" he asked.

Allison perked up, blinking her eyes. She chewed on her muffin and chased it with her French vanilla coffee. "Yeah, I'm fine. I'm just bored already. All my friends are out of town for spring break."

She knew inside, however, that it wasn't boredom eating at her brain. It was the constant images of the man from last night across from the park, loading the body into the trunk of that car. It was this dichotomy inside her, wanting to both forget and simultaneously remember every detail.

"Well, listen," Bobby said, setting down his iPad. "I have to be in Houston Monday morning to do a walkthrough on a new project, and I think Stephanie is going with me. So, we are going to leave tomorrow morning. I'm sure you and Lucas would be fine for one night by yourselves."

"You and mom are staying overnight?" Allison didn't want to sound concerned or paranoid, but the last thing she wanted was to be away from her parents or to be home by herself. She knew she needed to do something to get her mind occupied.

"Yeah, but we'll be back by dinner time on Monday."

"Have you told Lucas?"

"No, he's still over at Tyler's house. I figured we'd let him know when he comes home today." He could tell something more was on his daughter's mind. "Are you sure you're okay?"

"Yeah, Bobby. I'm fine, I promise." An idea popped into her head and it made her perk up. "I think I'll take Jake for a walk. It's nice outside and I could use some sunlight."

A golden retriever lying on a charcoal-colored dog bed in the living room popped his head up when he heard his name. The dog got up, shook his body, almost to wake up his joints and walked over to the kitchen breakfast bar. He sat at the side of Allison's barstool and laid his head on her lap.

"You want to go for a walk, old boy?" she said, scratching his head behind his ear. The dog licked her wrist as she pet him. "I'm going to get dressed and take him out."

Allison went back to her bedroom, pulled on a pair of black tights and a pair of old Nike running shoes. She found a purple Stephen F. Austin baseball cap and pulled her ponytail through the back.

With Jake's black nylon leash in hand, she told Bobby goodbye and walked out the front door. The mid-March morning air was crisp, with a hint of moisture; like the kind of morning when you know a thunderstorm is imminent that night. Now, however, the sun was shining with large puffy clouds creating shadows and cutting holes in the sunshine.

She really wasn't interested in taking the dog for a walk; it was just an excuse to go back to the park. Allison wanted to see the row of houses in the daylight—houses she'd seen her entire life but couldn't tell you what color they were. She found it amazing how few details you really paid attention to until you needed to. Looking out the fogged window of Brandon's Challenger, could she even be sure the car she saw was black? Were there any other details she could rack from her brain?

Nonetheless, she needed to go back. She needed to see the street and the parking lot where she and Brandon had hooked up. And a part of her hoped that the neighborhood across the street from the park was normal and fine. Of course, she didn't actually know that it was a body in that black trash bag. It could have been a dead animal. She tried to rationalize what she'd seen with every possible scenario. She wondered, with a macabre sense, how big Jake's body would look stuffed into that same black bag.

Jake tugged ahead on his leash and Allison tugged back to keep him at a comfortable pace. He sniffed around the sidewalks as they walked, stopping to pee on the occasional patch of grass or street-side pine tree. Marking his territory. Making it his. The golden retriever had been with their family since she was a little girl. He was a gift when Bobby and her mother found out they were pregnant with Lucas. Allison had essentially grown up with the dog. As she was becoming a woman, he was getting old. The hair around his eyes and snout were turning white in his advanced age. As much as she hated to admit it, she knew these kinds of walks had an expiration date to them.

They continued walking and turned the corner where the park was across from the house that she'd seen last night. There were two police cars parked out front of a house with white siding. One police officer was outside, leaning against his car while talking on his phone. He had the phone perched on one shoulder while writing notes on a notepad. A second officer, a female, her hair braided tight behind her head, was on the front porch of the house talking with a middle-aged Hispanic woman.

Allison lingered on the street corner and simply observed. It hit her in the pit of her stomach that if the police were involved, then her worst fears were correct—it was a body. She observed for a minute, the female cop talking with whom she assumed was the mother of the victim.

The mother.

If the woman on the front porch of the house was the mother, it was possible, Allison thought, that the person in the bag was close to her own age. The thought made her want to immediately turn around and go back home. She needed more information, however. She wanted to know details; to know that what she saw was real.

Allison took a deep breath and decided to go talk with the officer standing by the patrol vehicle. She approached the driver's side of the black Ford Mustang. The words Henderson PD were emblazoned across the doors and side panels.

As Allison walked forward, the officer, still on his cellphone said, "Let me call you right back, sir. I've got a young lady hear who looks like she wants to talk." He pressed the call to end and shoved the Samsung device into one of his many pockets on his uniform.

"What can I do for you, ma'am?" he asked. Allison looked at his chest. The name "Sullivan" was etched into a brass nametag on the left side of his uniform. He was tall, at least six feet, with broad shoulders and a strong jaw. A hint of stubble painted his cheeks and chin. Blonde hair, cut tight and high, peaked out from under his cap.

"Hi, Officer," Allison said. "I just," she stammered for a moment and then collected herself. "I was just taking my dog for a walk around the park and was interested in what's going on." She noticed the other officer and lady on the porch had their attention on her at this point.

"Well, I can't say much right now, actually," he said. Officer Sullivan motioned to the two women on the porch, asking his partner to come over.

The female officer came over. As she neared, Allison could tell she was older than the male officer, perhaps in her mid-thirties. Her brown hair was braided and tucked neatly under her cap. "Hi, I'm Officer Jones," she said, extending her hand. Allison shook it, the dog leash around her wrist. "I'm Allison."

"What's your last name, Allison? And how old are you?" Officer Jones asked.

"Hanes. And sixteen."

"So, you're what? A sophomore?"

"I'm a junior, ma'am. Graduating next year." Allison was starting to get nervous from all the questions and she was feeling a tinge of regret of coming over here. She thought that maybe this wasn't the best idea; that perhaps her curiosity may get her involved even more into a situation that she honestly wanted nothing of.

"Okay, that's good. Listen, do you know a girl named Ariel Perez at your school?"

Allison, in fact, did know Ariel. Ari, she was called, was a sophomore at Henderson High, but only because she was held back when they were in elementary school. They were the same age, however, and both played on the junior varsity volleyball team.

"I know of her, but I don't really hang out with her. Why?" But Allison already knew why.

"You wouldn't happen to know of any reason why she would have run away in the middle of the night? Any boyfriend trouble at school? Bullying, anything like that?"

"Not that I can think of," Allison said. She felt her palms starting to sweat. "Are you saying she ran away from home?" Allison hoped that by running with that theory—which the police obviously thought was the case—that she could avoid any further questions.

She wanted to help. She wanted to tell the officers what she'd seen. But at the same time, she knew that she couldn't, at least not yet. The last thing she wanted was to get involved in a case and have everything she'd been doing get out in the open.

"That seems to be the case," Officer Sullivan said. "We're just hoping someone close to her may know why."

"I can't think of anything. But like I said, I don't really know her that well," said Allison. "If you don't mind, officers, I need to get back home."

"Oh, absolutely." Officer Jones reached into a pocket on her shirt. "This is my card. If you hear anything about Ariel, or find out anything that could help us, would you give me a shout? My office number is on there as well as my email address." Allison took the card. It read Henderson Police Department Tina Jones, Detective with the phone number and email address underneath.

"Yes ma'am," Allison said. She pulled at the leash and Jake stood from a sitting position and came to her side. They walked away from the officers, back toward home. Allison was still nervous, and she wiped her sweaty palms on her shirt.

The two police officers watched as Allison walked away, the dog at her side.

"She knows something," Tina Jones said to Sullivan.

"What makes you think that?" her partner asked.

"I can just tell. She seemed nervous. Women's intuition."

"That's not a real thing, Jones. Kids get nervous talking to cops." Sullivan pulled the notepad he had been writing on out of his back pocket. "What did she say her name was? Allison Hayes?"

"Hanes. Allison Hanes." Officer Jones started walking back to the front porch where Ariel's mother was still standing, her hands folded across her chest, waiting for more information. "And let's go ahead and call in the Amber Alert."

CHAPTER SIX
SATURDAY MARCH 15 | 11:50AM

"IT'S GONE." LUCAS'S voice broke with fear and exhaustion. He tried to catch his breath. "Destroyed. Like a tornado hit it." He sat on the ground with a paper towel pressed to his bare knee poking through a rip in his jeans, the paper showing red with blood.

"Yeah, man." Tyler sat on the floor of Elijah's bedroom with his back against the door. Beads of sweat collected on his forehead and created lines down his temples. His dark skin glinted in the sunlight filtering through the bedroom window. "Freaking destroyed."

When Lucas and Tyler saw the destruction of the treehouse, they sprinted back through the woods to where their bikes were parked. Lucas had never felt such panic in his life. He had turned his head while running, to see the remains of the treehouse one more time, when he tripped over a branch. Falling face-first onto the forest floor, his skinned his knee against a piece of bark on the ground. His hands still stung from breaking his fall.

Tyler had helped him up to his feet and they continued, brushing by branches, the thin ones whipping against their arms and faces. Once they reached their bicycles, resting against a tree trunk, they picked them up and pumped their way back to Elijah's house. The whole ordeal was a blur. At one point, Lucas considered breaking away from his friend and just going home. The fleeting thought passed, however. He could not abandon Tyler.

They rolled up to Elijah's front yard, dumping the bikes on the grass. Both boys tumbled through the front door, shutting it and locking it behind them. Elijah's little sister sat in the living room eating cereal from a plastic bowl and watching a Disney cartoon on television and was unphased by their intrusion. The boys burst into Elijah's bedroom, where they sat now, breathless and afraid.

Elijah sat backward in his computer chair, his face twisted in disbelief. He interlocked his fingers above his head as he tried to calculate what his friends were telling him. "How? How is that possible?"

Tyler shook his head. "Whoever buried that body must have gone back to the fort and tore it down. Like, he wanted to make sure it was demolished. Keep us from going back out there." His words were disjointed as he caught his breath. He grabbed a plastic water bottle from his backpack, twisted off the cap and downed nearly the entire contents. "Which means," he said, catching his breath, "he knows we were there. He knows we saw him."

Lucas leaned back, his head resting against the wall. His breath was short and forced. He reached around for his own backpack and rustled around the internals until he found his asthma inhaler. He shook it, held it to his mouth and pumped twice while inhaling. "I don't know. I just..." His voice trailed off. Lucas's head drooped and he sighed. "I think we may have messed up here."

"Well, what can we do?" asked Elijah.

The emergency notification tone on Lucas's phone began going off. He pulled it out of his pocket. The notification bubble on the lock screen read AMBER ALERT Henderson, TX. No vehicle description. Check local media.

"Look, guys!" he said, perking up. He turned the phone screen to his friends. "This is from the news story this morning. The missing girl."

"So what?" Tyler said, standing up. "We can't do anything! Whoever did this, whoever took this girl, whoever buried that body in the woods, knows we saw!

Why else would they do that to our fort?" He was heated at this point, pacing across Elijah's bedroom floor. Sweat continued to drip down Tyler's temples.

"Yeah, Lucas," Elijah quipped. "We're just...we're just kids."

"Come on, guys!" Lucas pleaded. "We know something here!" Lucas didn't want to feel helpless. He wanted to feel like they could do something. "That guy, whoever he is, destroyed our fort because he wanted to scare us!"

"Well," Tyler said, "he's doing a damn good job of it because, I don't know about you, but I'm pretty scared. And at this point, I wouldn't even want to go back out to the fort."

"I don't either, man," Elijah said. "I mean, I was hoping last night that we could go back out there after this whole thing blows over. But man, there's a girl missing, and she's probably in that hole out there, and I don't want to go back near that place."

Lucas felt a tinge of pain in their words. All their hard work over the last three months; all the planning and excitement now lay in a heap on the forest floor. The planks and sheets of plywood were broken and destroyed by the same man who'd buried a body not even fifty yards from their treehouse.

Tyler turned to Lucas. "He's right, bro." He pointed to the iPhone still in Lucas's hand. "That girl, she's in the woods. She's in that hole."

"So, let's tell someone!" Lucas stood up. "Come on, guys. We can make this better. We can fix this! All we have to do is go to the cops. You guys said we could make a call if we saw something on the news today. Well, we saw something!"

Tyler walked over to his friend and put his hand on Lucas's shoulder. "I know, bro. I don't want to freak you out, but here's the thing; that guy destroyed our fort. He knows we were out there. And if he knows we were out there, who's to say he didn't watch us leave? What if he followed us and now he knows who we are? What if we go to the cops...and he comes after us?"

Lucas's breath caught in his throat. He hadn't thought of that. The idea of a killer watching them, possibly even now, filled him with even more dread. He looked at Elijah's bedroom window, paranoia taking over, to ensure the curtains were drawn.

He sat down on the beanbag chair on the ground and ran his hands through his hair. His hands felt clammy and his hair was full of dirt and sweat. Tyler sat down next to him and Elijah crossed the room to do the same.

"Let's just stick together right now," Tyler said. "Once the cops find the body, and they will soon, it'll all be okay. But until then, let's stick close. Right now, we're safe here at Elijah's house. We can go back to my house tonight."

"Hey guys, remember the whole TV forty-eight hours thing," Elijah said, hoping to bring some positivity to the situation. "That's not too long. Tyler's right. Let's stick together for the next few days and everything will be alright."

Lucas nodded and obliged, but internally was still feeling like they should be doing something. He knew these emotions would pass, especially if the crime scene was actually discovered soon. He conceded that they couldn't go back to the fort, but he just wanted to be able to enjoy spring break with his friends.

His phone buzzed again, and he pulled the device out of his pocket. It was a text from his dad. *I need you to come home*, it read. *Need to discuss something with you.*

"Oh no, guys," he looked up at Tyler and Elijah, who were firing up Fortnite on the Xbox. "I think we've been found out."

CHAPTER SEVEN
SATURDAY MARCH 15 | 1:00PM

LUCAS WALKED THROUGH the garage door of his house—the front door seemed more as decoration than an egress—and found his dad, Bobby, in the master bedroom. Lucas tried to remain calm, not wanting to give away any of his current nervousness. He worried that the fort had been discovered, or that he, Elijah, and Tyler had been found out somehow.

His fears were immediately squashed when his dad took him up in his arms, embracing his son in a bear hug. "Hey bud! How was your sleepover?" Bobby asked.

Lucas let out a sigh of relief. "It was good."

"Well, what did y'all do?"

"Oh, nothing really. Played video games."

Bobby released his son from the hug and went back

to his closet. Lucas watched as his dad piled a couple of polo shirts and jeans on the California king bed in the middle of the bedroom. ESPN played on the TV hung on the wall.

"Is everything okay?" Lucas asked, hoping to solicit some information, hoping that his parents were in the dark regarding the events of the last twelve hours.

"Oh yeah, why?"

"Oh. Well," Lucas paused, "I was just wondering why you're packing clothes."

Bobby looked down at the pile on the bed and chuckled. "Oh goodness. Yes, everything is fine. I wanted you to come home so I could tell you what's going on." As he spoke, Bobby went back to the walk-in closet and emerged into the bedroom carrying a black leather duffel bag. "I have a site walkthrough in Houston on Monday, and your mother is going with me, which means you and Allison will be alone tomorrow night."

"Oh." Lucas had never felt more relief in his life. As frightened as he was about the treehouse and the body in the woods, he felt like he was bought some time here. Even if the body was found soon, he figured that his parents would be in Houston during the immediate aftermath. "Well, Tyler asked if I could spend the night tonight."

Bobby folded a pair of jeans and stuffed them into

the duffel. "I thought that's where you were last night."

"Oh, I was," Lucas lied. "For a little bit. But we actually ended up going to Elijah's house because he got the new Fortnite update." That in itself wasn't a complete lie, he rationalized. There was a new Fortnite game update that all three boys were looking forward to playing. In fact, he knew that's what Tyler and Elijah were doing at this very moment.

"Gotcha. Well, just be sure you let me know where you are. So, yeah, you can spend the night with Tyler tonight after you clean your room though. I went in there earlier and it looks like a laundry bomb went off. Also, I'd prefer it if you stayed here tomorrow night. I don't like the idea of you or Allison out while we're gone, especially right now."

A lump formed in Lucas's throat. "What do you mean 'right now'?" Here it was again. Did his dad know something that he didn't? As close as the woods were to their neighborhood, he felt like he would have heard police sirens if the body had been found.

"It's not a big deal, and I don't want to scare you but there's a girl missing. She goes to school with your sister. She probably ran away from home, but just to be safe, I'd like for you two to stick around the house tomorrow until we get back." Bobby must have seen the worry on his son's face. He ruffled his son's hair.

"It's okay, bud. Between you and me, I don't think anything happened to her. She probably ran off with some boy she met on one of those phone apps. She'll show back up soon, I'm sure. Who knows, probably today."

Lucas hopped onto the bed and swung his feet over the wooden footboard. He continued watching his dad packed the duffel with his clothes for the trip. "So what are you building in Houston?" he asked, changing the subject from the missing girl.

"We're building a new hospital down there in one of the suburbs, and we're just doing a walkthrough of the project so far. It should be done and complete by August, so we'll have to go back a couple of times this summer."

Bobby had been in the construction industry Lucas's entire life, and longer. These kinds of trips were not uncommon, but this was the first time that his mom, Stephanie, had gone with Bobby overnight. Which meant it was also the first the first time Lucas and Allison would be left alone overnight while their parents were out of town.

Lucas felt a tinge of pride in that fact. He liked that his parents felt that they could trust them to be by themselves. That feeling was fleeting, however, as anxiety started to creep into the boy's mind. He tried to push it away. Deep down, despite the current situation, he knew that he could be trusted. And, frankly, he was tired of thinking about what he and his friends had seen. Maybe Tyler was right – the police would be on the case and the body would be found.

Deciding to forget all about the treehouse and the body, he looked up at his dad with a mischievous grin. "So, dad, how many people can I have at my party tomorrow night?"

ANDREW J BRANDT

CHAPTER EIGHT
SATURDAY MARCH 15 | 3:02PM

ALLISON'S PHONE WAS inundated with messages about Ariel from her friends. A Netflix series droned in the background on her TV mounted above her vanity. She laid on her bed, the Tiffany-blue sheets and comforter a mess around her, reading. Her phone straight up in the air above her head, she scrolled through the messages between an iMessage group and different Snapchat threads. Instagram was full of "Come home Ariel" posts and "We love you Ariel" comments under pictures of a girl who Allison knew, for all intents and purposes, would not be coming home.

A text from her best friend Amilyn came through. *I wish I was home so I could be with you right now.* Allison wished she was as well. If anything, she wanted someone to cry on, to open up to. Someone who wouldn't judge her for her choices. Or, more appropriately, she wished she'd been allowed to go with Amilyn to San Antonio for the weekend. However, Bobby and her mother thought it inappropriate for her to be away without adult supervision in another city with three other high school girls. But, at this point she wished she'd put up a fight, argued her case a little more persistently. The girls would have stayed at Amilyn's older sister's apartment, who was technically an adult. They didn't budge, however. But if they had, if she'd been allowed to go, then perhaps she would have been just as perplexed about Ariel Perez's disappearance as everyone else in Henderson.

I wish I could be with you! I hope you're having fun! Allison typed back to Amilyn. She decided to keep her inner turmoil just that for now—inner.

She watched the three dots on her screen and waited for Amilyn's response. A few seconds later, her phone dinged. *We are having fun. Would be much better with you here.*

How's the riverwalk? Allison typed out.

OMG girl it's so pretty. We need to plan a trip this summer. They have a minor league baseball team. And I know how much you love those boys in baseball pants lol.

This made Allison smile, the blue message bubbles

going back and forth. She didn't feel so alone now.

Coming home soon?

Tomorrow.

Perf. My parents are leaving for Houston in the morning.

Oooh girl. Gonna get you some Brandon lovin'?

Stopppppp.

Lol. see you tomorrow love.

There was a knock at her bedroom door. Her mother cracked it open. "You taking a nap, sweetie?"

Allison shoved her phone under her pillow and sat up on her bed. "No, just watching some Netflix. How was your showing this morning?"

Stephanie Beaker stepped in. She was still in her business dress, a black dress that accentuated her hips. Even in her mid-forties, she still had a youthful body and figure. The only thing, really, that gave away her age were the wisps of grey beginning to show up in the part of her otherwise dark shoulder-length hair.

"I think they're going to buy, actually," she said. "Which is good. Momma needs to sell some houses." She sat down on the edge of Allison's bed. Her daughter scooted over a few inches to give her some room.

Stephanie Beaker was fairly new to the real estate game. She'd had a couple of secretarial jobs when she was younger, the longest as a receptionist at a law office downtown. She'd quit working for several years after Lucas was born, but between a mix of boredom and wanting to capitalize on a hot market, she decided to dive head-first into real estate. She'd sold four homes her first year and seven her second. Now in her third year, she was becoming a known-name in the industry. "Do Better With Beaker!" was the slogan on her business cards.

Allison looked up at her mother. "Mom, has anything bad ever happened in Henderson?"

"Oh, honey. Are you worried about Ari?"

"I mean, a little bit. What if she didn't run away? What if something bad happened to her?"

"Well, from what I've heard through the grapevine—you know how word travels around this town— is that there wasn't anything out of the ordinary at her house. No signs of struggle, no blood or anything like that. She very likely just walked out the front door and went somewhere. Probably ran off with some boy she met in Nacogdoches. I hear she was pretty promiscuous."

"No she wasn't, Mom," Allison said defensively. She caught herself talking about Ari in the past tense, like it was a foregone conclusion. "I mean, she's not. Ari's a good girl."

What Allison really wanted was to confide in her mother, to tell her that Ari, in fact, didn't walk out of her house last night. That she was carried out, in a trash bag. She couldn't bring herself to do it though. It would expose her, and her relationship with Brandon.

"Has anyone ever been kidnapped here though?"

"Not that I know of. This is a pretty safe little town. Of course, every little place has their seedy pasts and underbellies. But I think the most controversial thing to ever happen here was when Nancy Wallace got caught sleeping with the DA."

Small town gossip was something Stephanie excelled at, Allison knew. And gossip traveled fast in a town of less than fifteen thousand. It wasn't rare for her mother and the other women in the neighborhood, or women in her real estate sales group, to be found at the dining room table, bottles of wine strewn about. Their voices, getting louder and louder as the wine kept flowing, all talking about "Oh my god, did you hear about…" and "You won't believe who I saw…"

"Here's the thing, babe," Stephanie took her daughter's hand. "If that little girl was actually taken from her home, somebody would have seen it. This town is too small for a secret like that to stay quiet."

ANDREW J BRANDT

CHAPTER NINE
SATURDAY MARCH 15 | 7:27PM

LUCAS FINISHED CLEANING his bedroom after dinner, as requested by his parents, and threw a clean pair of jeans and a T-shirt into his backpack. While putting his clothes in, he pulled out the Avengers poster, still rolled up from the boys' abandonment of the treehouse. While this morning he wanted to be a hero, now he just wanted to be a kid. He kept the poster furled up and placed it on a shelf in his closet next to a modest collection of comic books. His interests had changed over the last year, in the transition from elementary to middle school, and where there were once toys and action figures in his bedroom, he now had posters and comic books.

Hey I'm headed over, he texted to Tyler.

Okay cool. Elijah's already here. He brought his Xbox.

73

He shut off his bedroom light and walked out to the living room. "I'm going to Tyler's, dad," he said. Bobby was sitting on the living room couch, watching a spring training baseball game.

"Okay, kiddo. Text me when you get there."

"Yes sir," Lucas said.

Pumping his bicycle out of the driveway and into the street, Lucas turned the corner on Dogwood street toward Tyler's house. The early spring air was cool, and he wished he'd put on his favorite Spiderman hoodie, but he decided that he could tough out the four-block bike ride over to his friend's house in just his long sleeve Henderson Lions high school football t-shirt. The sun was already below the horizon, the sky painted in hues of pink and orange above him. Some of the brighter stars were already visible toward the west. The oak trees that lined the residential streets would eventually create a green blanket above the street, but for now the limbs were either still bare or new leaves were just budding.

As Lucas pumped down Dogwood in the dusk, his backpack bouncing against his back, he noticed headlights from a car shining behind him. He leaned his bicycle closer to the curb to allow the car to pass, but it never did. He could see his shadow in front of him, elongated and stretched out on the pavement. Lucas turned his head to see why the car hadn't passed him yet, hoping that the driver had pulled up to a house and parked on the curb. The car, however, was still driving along, following him. It was a black sedan, the emblem on the silver grill read "Ford" in a blue pendant.

Lucas pedaled faster now, and the car kept pace. He peeked over his shoulder again and the car revved its engine. Terror gripped Lucas as he stood up on his pedals and pumped them as quickly as his legs would allow.

The car revved again, inching closer to the boy, the headlights getting closer, making Lucas's shadow shorten in length. Mustering every bit of strength he had, Lucas pedaled harder, his calves and lungs both burning.

He turned his head once again and the car was right behind him, no more than five yards between his back tire and the front fender of the vehicle. Lucas decided his only recourse was to get off the street. He remembered something he'd learned in school last year; during a presentation about stranger danger, there was a scenario where a young girl in Oklahoma had evaded a potential kidnapping by riding her bike up to a random house on her street and pretended she lived there.

With the car barreling on him, Lucas hopped the curb to his right and rode up onto the sidewalk, threading two oak trees lining the street. He pedaled up into the driveway of a nondescript red-brick house, its garage set back off the street.

He dumped the bike into some shrubbery next to the house and watched from behind the branches between the house and garage as the car sped off toward Kilgore Drive. As it drove away, he noticed the passenger side tail light was taped over like it had been broken, and instead of replacing it, they just covered it with red tape. He sat in the shrubs, waiting for the black car to come back down the street but he felt safe to be able to continue on to Tyler's house. Finally, he stood up, dusted the dirt and grass from his jeans and pulled his bicycle up out of the shrubs. The sky was nearly full dark now, but the streetlights had not yet come on.

* * *

"I was pretty freaked out. I don't know what their deal was," Lucas said to his dad. He sat on the black leather sectional at Tyler's house, tucked under the crook of his dad's arm. His mother sat on the other side of him, with Tyler's parents, John and Victoria, on the outstretched end of the couch. Tyler sat on the armrest next to them.

When he arrived at their house, he didn't even bother knocking, crashing through the front door. When he told Tyler's parents what had happened, they immediately called Bobby and Stephanie, who drove over without hesitation. Now, the six of them sat in the Washington family living room.

"He said he didn't get a good look at the driver," John said. "But we'll put a bolo out on the vehicle description. Probably some kid being an asshole." Victoria lightly tapped her husband on the thigh to remind him to watch his language.

Bobby looked at his son, "Well, do you want to just come back home tonight? We can put your bike in the back of the truck."

"No, I think I'll be fine," Lucas said.

"We don't mind him staying. He's more than welcome and safe here," said Victoria. "Besides, dinner is almost ready, and I'm sure you could use some food in your belly after all that."

Lucas nodded, and he could smell the food in the oven, a pan of chicken and vegetables roasting, its aromas filling the air.

"What do you think, babe?" Bobby asked Stephanie.

If he's okay now, I think it's fine."

They all stood up, Bobby and Stephanie shaking hands with and thanking the Washingtons. John Washington towered over all of them, even Bobby, at over six feet tall. Lucas's mom leaned him to hug her son when John's cellphone rang from the other room.

"Hang on one second, guys," he said, excusing himself. "Let me get this."

He went over to the kitchen counter where his phone was resting on the charger. "This is Officer Washington," he answered. He listened to the speaker on the other end of the connection. "Okay. Yes sir. I'll be right there." He hung up and placed the device in his pocket.

"Everything okay, honey?" his wife asked.

He looked up, pursing his lips with a hint of defeat in his eyes and sighed. "I have to go in. They think they found that missing girl's phone."

CHAPTER TEN
SATURDAY MARCH 15 | 10:43PM

THE WINDOW IN Tyler's bedroom faced the street, and Lucas peered out, knowing that at any moment that black car would drive by, hunting for him. He was still shaking from the earlier altercation, and his friends did their best to ensure him that it was safe now.

"I'm telling you, guys, it was the man in the woods. He's found us. Like you said, Tyler. He followed us from the treehouse. Now he knows where we live." Lucas said.

"We're safe here, though," Tyler said. "There's no way that dude is going to mess with my dad."

Tyler's favorite basketball team, the Houston Rockets, were playing on the TV, but none of the boys could focus enough to pay attention to the game. They kept finding their attention focused on the window, peeping out the white blinds that covered the window.

Tyler's father had been gone for over two hours, and they kept waiting and listening for the garage door to open, signaling his arrival. Lucas did his best to hide the fear from his parents when they came over earlier, but he knew that he, along with his friends, would feel much safer with Mr. Washington back home. At the same time, however, they hoped that the police finding the missing girl's phone meant that they had more clues into finding whoever it was that took her and that they were close to catching the perp.

"Well, if it is the same guy, we need to find that car. Like a stakeout or something," Lucas said. "We should bait him into following one of us again and set him up."

"He almost ran me over last time," Lucas said. "So I don't know if I want to take my chances again."

"We need a plan for sure," said Elijah. "He took out our treehouse and now he's chasing Lucas around our own neighborhood. This is the most screwed up spring break ever."

"Oh, and don't forget there's a dead girl out in the woods," Tyler said. "So, this guy is crazy. I just don't know why he'd be coming after us."

Lucas looked out the window again. "Maybe he wants us to be scared. He doesn't want us going to the cops and telling them what we saw out there."

"You're probably right. But we need to get this guy. I'm not going to spend my entire life looking over my shoulder waiting to get ran over by some crazy dude," Tyler said. "I say tomorrow, we start looking for him."

"What are we going to do though, Tyler?" Lucas asked, his voice perturbed and anxious. "We're kids. The best thing we can do is tell the cops, tell your dad, what we saw out there."

"And spend the rest of sixth grade grounded? Heck no, bro. I can handle him destroying the fort. But he's coming after us now? This is personal." Tyler was getting heated.

"Guys let's stay calm and focused," Elijah interjected. "We won't solve anything getting angry. And I agree, we can't go to the cops, at least not yet. Lucas, you sure you didn't get the license plate number?"

Lucas hung his head dejectedly, "No. I wish I would have. I know that's what they tell us at school, that we're supposed to look for that, but honestly, in the moment, I was so scared. I just knew I needed to get off the street."

"I don't blame you, bro," Tyler said. He sat next to Lucas on the floor. "We're here for you though. And we're going to get him, whoever he is."

"So what do you think we should do?" Lucas asked.

Elijah said, "I say we get back out there tomorrow

and ride around and find this car. What did you say it was? A Ford?"

"Yeah, a black Ford car," Lucas said.

"This town isn't that big," Tyler said. "We'll find it. And if all three of us are together, I don't think the guy would mess with us in the broad daylight."

As the boys were talking, they heard the garage door, the mechanical sound of the automatic opener pulling the double-sized door on its chain. It was the sound of Tyler's father returning from his call-in duty.

The door leading into the house opened and they heard John toss his keys onto the kitchen counter. The three boys went out into the kitchen to find out what happened with the missing girl's cell phone.

Victoria came in and hugged her husband. "What's going on, honey?" she asked.

"Well, it's definitely her phone," he said, removing his blue sportscoat. "It was destroyed, broken in half. They're going to take it back into the crime lab for analysis."

"Where was it?" his wife asked.

"Near one of the trails out in the woods, just a few blocks over. They're sending out a search crew to see if she's out there."

Victoria Jones hugged her husband, and he held her tight, the three boys standing in the doorway, watching silently.

"If I were a betting man," John said, "I'd say she's buried out there somewhere."

CHAPTER ELEVEN
SUNDAY MARCH 16 | 12:10AM

THE iPHONE VIBRATED against the wood surface of Allison's bedside table, startling her. She unlocked the screen to read the text message *I'm here* from Brandon. He had parked around the block a few houses down so his car couldn't be heard as he approached the Beaker home. She had the art of sneaking in and out of this window down to a science. Allison even knew the blind spots in the cameras positioned outside the house. Their home sat on a corner lot, and the garage and house formed an L-shape. There was one camera above the two-car garage, facing south. Another camera faced west from the front porch. Her bedroom window nearly faced southwest, but it was far enough from each camera that if Brandon crossed the street from the house caddy-corner from her window, he wouldn't trip the motion sensors on the devices.

She went to her bedroom window and unlatched the locks. Slowly, she lifted the window so as not to make any noise and waited for Brandon to come up to it. He hoisted himself up on and through the window sill. When he came in like this at night, they always kept the window open in case he needed to escape quickly.

"Hey," he said. He took her up in his arms and kissed her. She felt his hands around the small of her back, holding her tight. She wanted to stay there in his embrace in the soft glow of her bedside lamp. Her walls, painted a light grey, gave off a cool vibe. She had a song from The Maine playing on an Echo device on her bedside table.

"I have to tell you, I went back to the park today," Allison said with a sigh, her cheek resting against Brandon's chest. He pulled away from her.

"What? Why?"

"I don't know." She hung her head. "I couldn't get it out of my head, and I guess I wanted to know for certain that it was a body that that guy put in the trunk of the car." Her eyes welled up with tears. "And it was. It was Ari, from volleyball."

"The little one? The libero? How do you know?"

"When I walked down there this morning, the police were at her house. They were talking with her mom."

"Did you talk to the cops?" he inquired with a hint of exasperation in his voice.

"I just asked them what was going on. They think Ari ran away. One of the officers gave me her card, told me to call her if I heard anything from any of our friends." Allison removed herself from Brandon's arms and walked over to her computer desk. She pulled open the drawer and showed him the business card Officer Jones had given her. "But we know, Brandon. We know she didn't run away. She was in that trash bag. That man threw her in the trunk of that car like trash." Allison was crying full on at this point yet trying to remain as quiet as possible so as not to wake her parents. She sunk onto her computer chair, her shoulders and chest heaving with every breath.

She continued to sob for a few moments and then collected herself. "I've been trying to point my finger on what I'm feeling, and I finally figured it out. It's guilt. I feel guilty for seeing what we saw, and not saying anything."

"I know, babe, I get it," Brandon walked over and knelt beside the computer chair. He took her hands in his own. "I just don't want you, or me, to do or say something that could affect us as well. I know that sounds selfish, I know." He continued to caress her hands. "We have a lot at stake here too. I can't stand the thought of not being able to see you anymore."

In some way, this made Allison feel better. She definitely didn't want to lose what she had with Brandon either.

He continued, "I'm sorry we were at the park last night, and I'd give anything for us to have not seen what we saw. I'd give anything for you to not feel this way. I love you, babe. I don't want you to hurt. But we need to be quiet, at least for a little bit. This is a small town. Not much happens here without the whole town knowing about it. She'll be found soon, I promise."

She sniffed and wiped her eyes on the sleeve of her t-shirt. "You're right. I still feel like we could be doing something. Anything."

Brandon looked up in Allison's eyes. He reached up and wiped a tear rolling down her cheek. "I have an idea," he said. "We could call in an anonymous tip. We could at least give them the car that the guy was in. What was it? A Ford?"

Her eyes widened. "Yes! A black Ford. With four doors. A sedan. Oh my god, Brandon."

"What?" he asked.

"That black Ford! Earlier tonight, Lucas called my stepdad, scared out of his mind because a car was chasing him when he was biking over to his friend's house. He said it was a little black Ford."

"Is he okay?" Brandon's looked at her in disbelief, not able to comprehend the coincidence.

"Yeah, he was just freaked out. But it could be the same car! Why would they try to scare Lucas like that?"

"I'm not sure; maybe they were just being reckless. It may not have been the same car. But, you're right." he said. "All we have to do is call in an anonymous tip, tell the cops that a black four-door sedan is connected to Ariel's disappearance. Surely there aren't too many of those in this town." His voice sounded confident and sure.

"You'd be surprised," she said, "but there are probably more of those than matte black Challengers." She smiled at her own joke and Brandon was glad she could bring some levity to the conversation.

"That's the spirit. Like I said, babe. It'll all be fine." He kissed her and she kissed him back, wrapping her arms around his shoulders. The continued making out for a few minutes, their hands exploring each other's bodies. His lips made their way down her neck and to her chest as he wrapped her body in his arms.

He lifted her up and carried her to the bed.

* * *

Brandon pulled his phone out of his pocket to check the time. It read 12:52am. "I've got to get going, babe," he said. He lifted himself off her bed and pulled on his jeans. Allison wrapped herself in the soft Tiffany-blue comforter and perched up on one arm.

"Thank you for coming over tonight," she said. "And thank you for letting me cry. I love you."

"Of course, babe. Anything for you." He pulled his shirt over his head and leaned down to kiss her again.

"I've got baseball drills tomorrow and then I've got to help my dad at the store in the evening."

"Well, my parents are leaving for Houston in the morning," Allison said with a wink. "They'll be gone til Monday evening. After Lucas goes to bed, we could…" she trailed off. But he knew what she meant. And it got him imagining it already, even though he'd just had her. He already couldn't wait to not have to worry about parents or being quiet.

"I can't wait," he said. He kissed her again, walked to the window and swung his body out into the open. He pulled the glass panel window down slowly and made sure it was shut all the way, knowing that Allison would get up out of the bed to secure the locks and close the blinds. Once it was shut, he blew her a kiss through the window and started to make his way back to his car. He ensured there were no cars driving by that would or could see him leaving Allison's window and crossed the street.

He made a slight jog to the vehicle and fished for his keys in the front pocket of his jeans. He used the key to unlock the door as opposed to the keyless entry; no need to flash the headlights or bring any unnecessary attention to his car parked in front of some stranger's house. His biggest fear doing this with Allison was that he'd go back and find an empty spot where his car once was, towed away thanks to some unscrupulous and nosey neighbor.

However tonight, the Dodge Challenger was right where he left it. He dropped into the driver's seat, put the key in the ignition and started it up. When he looked up to make sure his headlights didn't turn on, he saw something, a piece of paper, under the windshield wiper. He opened the car door, reached up and grabbed it. It was a scrap of notebook paper, ripped from a spiral instead of the loose-leaf type, the frayed edges still attached to the perforation. It was a note, written in Sharpie.

In the light from the bulb above his head he read the note, scribbled in all caps:

I KNOW YOU SAW ME. I HAVE SEEN YOU TO. IF YOU GO TO THE COPS SHE IS NEXT.

CHAPTER TWELVE
SUNDAY MARCH 16 | 11:10AM

ALLISON AWOKE TO a loud, incessant pounding at the front door. Still delirious from sleep, it took her a moment to remember she was the only person home to answer the door. She got up out of bed, pulled on a sweater and walked down the hall to the front door.

She looked out the view hole in the door to see Brandon standing on her front porch, his Challenger parked on the curb. She opened the door and he nearly barreled her over. Brandon shut the door behind him and peered out the peephole. "Making sure I wasn't followed," he said.

"Followed? By who? You're scaring me, babe, what's going on?"

"I've been calling you all morning. And texting you. You never answered so I left baseball practice. I needed to make sure you're safe." He turned to face Allison. "Are you here by yourself?" he asked. She said yes, that her parents had left early in the morning.

"Why? What's going on?"

"You're not safe here," he said. He checked the lock on the door. "Is your window locked?"

At this point, Allison was both scared and confused. "Brandon, what the hell are you doing? Why are you freaking out?"

He reached into his pocket and pulled out a crumpled piece of paper. "Last night when I left, this was on my car."

She opened up the note and read it. She felt the color drain from her face. "Oh my god, Brandon."

"Yeah, babe. I know."

"Oh my god," she repeated, louder and panicked. "What the hell? What are we going to do?"

"Well for one, we are getting you out of here. You can't stay here by yourself. Where's your brother? Is he home with you?"

"No, he's at Tyler's house," she said.

"Isn't his dad a cop?" Brandon asked.

Allison nodded yes. She read the note again, the block letters written in thick black marker, the edges of the paper torn and uneven.

"Okay, that's good," he said. "Make sure he stays there. You, though, we need to get you somewhere

where you're not alone for tonight. Is Amilyn still in San Antonio?"

"She's coming home today."

"Perfect," he said, walking down the hallway. As he went, he walked into every room, checking the latches on the windows. "We can keep the windows and doors locked and hole up here until she gets into town."

"Brandon, if he comes for me, what's going to stop him? I mean, he took Ari. He can just as easily take me."

Brandon lifted his shirt and showed her a black pistol tucked into the waistband of his jeans. "It's my dad's. I took it out of his safe." He pulled his shirt back down, obscuring the weapon.

"Jesus, Brandon!" Allison was in shock at this point. A madman, who had already killed one girl, was threatening to take her, and now her boyfriend had a gun in his pants. "What are you even doing with that thing?"

"I'm not going to let anything happen to you," he said. "I don't know who this guy is, but if he thinks he's going to come after my girlfriend, he's going to go down."

Finally, after he'd checked all the windows and door locks, Brandon took Allison in his arms and embraced her. She could feel the pistol pressing against her pubic bone. "I love you," he said. "And I'm going to protect you, no matter what."

"I love you. But I'm definitely scared," she said. "I almost wish you hadn't showed me that note."

"I know, but I needed you to know how serious this is. This guy, he knows who we are, and he knows we saw him take Ari." He released her from the embrace. "It'll be okay. We'll be fine as long as we stay here."

"I need to text Lucas. My parents wanted him to come home this morning, so I need him to stay with the Joneses for the day." She went back to her bedroom and grabbed her phone off her bedside table. She quickly thumbed out a message to Lucas. I've got to take some clothes to a friend. Stay at Tyler's for a little while. She also sent one to Amilyn. Let me know when you get back into town. I need to see you ASAP.

She found a scrunchy on her computer desk and pulled her hair through it, making a messy ponytail. Since she and Brandon would be bunkered in the house, she didn't feel any need or desire to get dressed any further than her joggers and sweater. Allison walked back into the living room where Brandon was sitting on the couch. He looked up at her and smiled. "Damn girl, you are so fine."

She went to sit next to him, curling her legs underneath her body. "I'm literally in sweats. I'm as un-fine as you can get." She was cut off when she heard the sirens.

Police sirens were approaching the house. They

looked at each other and immediately hopped up and went to the front door. Brandon opened the door and they looked outside just as two police cruisers drove by unusually fast. They watched as the two cruisers turned down Dogwood Lane, both cars with sirens and lights blaring.

Brandon looked at Allison, a smile forming on his face. "You know what that means? I bet they got him."

CHAPTER THIRTEEN
SUNDAY MARCH 16 | 10:02AM

LUCAS PEDALED HIS bicycle on a dark road, breathing heavy, trying to get to the light in front of him. He knew if he could reach the light, he would be safe. He pedaled hard, his thighs burning from the effort. The trees above his head had black branches and they drooped down, almost touching the top of his head.

Behind him, the black car roared. The headlights grew brighter as the vehicle approached and gained on the boy.

With every ounce of effort in his body, Lucas pumped the pedals on his bicycle, but no matter how much he tried, he wasn't gaining speed. Looking behind him, he saw the black car just as its front fender hit his back tire.

Lucas flew into the air from the impact, his arms flailing in front of him. He landed not in the street, but in the woods. He stood up and dusted the dirt off his jeans and shirt. His hands were scraped and bleeding.

The sound of a shovel slicing into the ground behind him made him turn around. He saw a dark figure digging into the earth. It was wearing a black hoodie, its face hidden beneath the hood. It looked up at Lucas with glowing red eyes. Lucas tried to run but his legs were paralyzed with fear.

Elijah and Lucas lay motionless on the ground in front of the hole. Their shirts and jeans were ragged and torn like they'd been dragged through the woods, their clothing catching on every branch and rock. Lucas realized that they were dead.

The figure pointed at him; its hand outstretched from the hoodie's sleeves was only bones. "You're next," it growled. "I'm coming for you, Lucas Beaker."

* * *

Lucas's jumped awake. His eyes darted around the bedroom and he realized he had been dreaming. Tyler and Elijah were still asleep, both boys in their sleeping bags. They had made a pallet of blankets on the floor of Tyler's bedroom and slept there. Tyler must have felt Lucas jump awake because he mumbled for a moment and turned over, falling back asleep.

Falling back onto his pillow, Lucas sighed. It had been a nightmare, but his heart still raced from the fear. He shook the images from his mind. It was just a dream, he told himself, repeating the words in his mind like a chant.

His throat felt rough and dry and he got out of his sleeping bag to go to the kitchen for a glass of water. Tyler's mom was in there already, pouring a cup of coffee from the carafe on the counter. Whereas Mr. Washington was tall and large, built like a linebacker, his wife was tall yet petite. Lucas could see where Tyler got his lankiness.

"Hi Mrs. Washington," Lucas said. "I was just wanting some water."

"Oh, sure thing," she said. She walked over to the refrigerator and pulled open one of the double stainless-steel doors. She twisted the cap to release the plastic and offered the boy a bottle of Ozarka water.

"Thank you," he said as he gulped it down.

"You're so welcome." Victoria moved to sit at the dining room table, coffee in one hand and phone in the other. "Are you okay? Did you boys stay up too late?" she asked as she sipped her brew.

"No ma'am. We watched basketball and then played Fortnite for a little bit." During the evening, the boys played the video game to try to distract them from the mysterious black car and the body in the woods. It had worked mostly, as they did stay up past midnight in a battle royale, the game's massive multiplayer contest.

He took another sip from the water bottle. "Do you think they're going to find that missing girl soon?" Lucas was hoping he could extract some information about the missing girl, specifically what the police currently knew about the situation.

"I certainly hope so," she said. She continued sipping her coffee and scrolling through her phone. "But we'll see. I think them finding her phone is a big piece of the puzzle."

"Why do you say that?" Lucas tried to sound concerned and now show any excitement that his plan was working.

"Well, it should be able to tell us who she was talking with or texting. Maybe she was planning on meeting up with someone. We don't really know a whole lot of details. But John and his guys are out there now, combing the area for any more clues."

"Wow," Lucas said. "So, they're out in the woods?"

"Yes, out in the area where they found her phone."

"Well, I hope they find something. Thank you again for the water."

"Of course, sweetheart. If you need anything else, let me know."

Lucas went back into Tyler's bedroom. Both Tyler and Elijah were waking up. "Tyler, your dad is back out there," he nodded toward the window, "with the investigation. If all the police are working in the woods, then we can go find that car."

Tyler stood up from the floor and stretched. "Let's do it, bro. Let's find where he's hiding out at and we can call the cops to arrest him."

Elijah said, "We need a plan. Where do we start?"

Lucas grabbed his backpack off the floor and found his phone inside one of the external pockets. "Let's think. Where did she live?" He opened up the Henderson newspaper website again in his browser, but the story didn't have any information about her residence.

"Wasn't she the same age as your sister?" Tyler asked. "Do you think she would have known her?"

"Maybe," Lucas said. "Allison's friends come over a lot, but I've never seen this girl. So I don't think they're friends."

Tyler said, "What if we start by the area and houses close to the woods? Maybe the guy dropped her out there because it's close to where he lives."

That made sense to Lucas. "Let's try that first. There's probably going to be a lot of cops out there too, though, if that's where they found her phone."

"Well, let's quit wasting time," Elijah piped up. "Let's find him while the case is hot."

The three boys got dressed quickly, excited to be doing something instead of hiding out in their bedrooms. They knew it would still be on the colder side outside in the morning so they each threw on a sweatshirt with their jeans.

They exited the bedroom and saw Tyler's mom still at the dining room table working on her cup of coffee.

"Hey mom, we were going to the park to play some football. Is that okay?"

"Do you have your phone on you?" she asked.

"Yes ma'am. We'll be safe. We just want to get out of the house for a little bit."

She obliged their request, and the boys hurried out to the garage, mounted their bicycles and rode off toward the part of the neighborhood that faced the woods. The morning air was thick with fog, which was common in the spring. It usually cleared out as the sun rose higher in the sky.

"Hey Lucas," Elijah shouted. He was riding slightly behind Lucas, with Tyler leading the pack. "If you see a car that looks even close to the one from the other night, take a picture of the license plate!"

"Good idea!" Lucas said. He was trying to keep the image fresh in his mind, the shape of the front fender and the headlights, hoping he'd be able to make it out easily if they saw it again. "I'll let you guys know if I see it," he called out.

They pedaled on, looking into the driveways of the houses on the block, but didn't see anything that even resembled a black Ford car. Behind them, the sirens of a police car sounded and Lucas noticed the noise getting louder. Two cop cars turned the corner behind them and rapidly approached.

The boys pulled their bikes over to the sidewalk and the police cruisers passed them, lights and sirens loud in the otherwise quiet neighborhood.

Tyler said, "I bet they found him! Let's go!" He pulled his bike back into the street and started in the direction the cops went, following their sirens. Lucas and Elijah quickly followed.

As Lucas pumped his pedals, he felt a sense of relief, hoping they'd get to see the perpetrator in handcuffs. His anticipation turned to unease when he realized they were heading toward the clearing in the woods where they would hike to the treehouse.

They turned the corner where the neighborhood butted against the woods. There they saw several police units around the clearing where the trails led into the forest. Tyler hit his brakes and Elijah and Lucas followed suit. Their tires left black skid marks on the asphalt. Before them was a full-on crime scene investigation.

Yellow police tape roped off the area. There were at least ten officers, including local police as well as a dispatch of Texas Rangers, standing around. Even a K9 dog unit was present. There was also an ambulance. Lucas realized very suddenly that they had not found the perpetrator at all. All this was for something different, something worse. His stomach dropped and a lump formed in his throat.

The three boys stood on their bicycles in the middle of the street and watched silently as a gurney was loaded into the back of an ambulance by EMTs.

Laying atop the gurney was a body wrapped in black plastic.

PART TWO
THE MAN IN THE BLACK CAR

CHAPTER FOURTEEN
WEDNESDAY MARCH 19 | 2:45PM

LUCAS REACHED TWO fingers under the collar of his shirt and scratched at his neck. The collar and tie made his skin itch. He wasn't used to wearing this kind of clothing very often, except for maybe Easter. He sat next to his sister, who had tears streaming down her face and his mom and dad, both silent and stoic. The memorial service for Ariel was held at the community center, which most often hosted the homecoming dance and senior prom. In fact, not even the largest church in Henderson, First Baptist, could hold the considerable amount of people who showed up today. Folded chairs were aligned in dozens of rows, and nearly a hundred more people standing in the back of the room. Even the atrium was full, with people over-flowing out the open doors.

Instead of a casket, a large spray of purple and white

flowers with the girl's picture in the middle was displayed at the front of the assembly room. The high school choir lead the congregation in singing a selection of worship songs before the eulogy, given by the preacher of the church the girl attended. Pastor Daniel was a young charismatic man in his mid-40's wearing dark jeans, a tailored white button-up and blazer. As he spoke to those in attendance about comfort and peace in this particularly heavy and tumultuous time, he kept his gaze often on the girl's family.

The family, taking up the first couple of rows, could be heard bawling even in the back. Lucas could see them, the mother crying on someone's shoulder. Lucas looked around the room, not really knowing what to do except listen to the preacher.

A few rows in front of him, he could see Tyler and his parents. Elijah, his mom and little sister were standing in the back somewhere. Almost as if he could sense Lucas looking at him, Tyler turned around and locked eyes with Lucas. Tyler gave him a slight head nod and Lucas raised his hand to say hello.

He hadn't seen Tyler in a couple of days. The day Ariel's body was found, Stephanie Beaker drove back to Henderson from Houston. His dad still had to work, but carpooled back to town with someone else from their firm the next day. The last seventy-two hours had been a whirlwind and a blur. When the girl's death was ruled a homicide, and no leads or suspects, most parents feared the worst.

Couple the paranoia of a possible murderer on the loose with the fact that some madman had tried to run over Lucas over the weekend, and he was on, what felt like to him, house arrest.

Allison had stayed holed up in her room as well, and Lucas assumed the death of her classmate hit his sister hard emotionally. He couldn't imagine someone he went to school with being murdered.

He also felt a tinge of guilt. Sitting here, listening to the eulogy and memorial of the girl's life, he felt like he could have done something sooner. He wondered if the murderer would have or could have been caught by now had he and his friends spoken up about what they'd seen out in the woods that first night.

No one, including the police, had quite put together that the man in the black car that had chased him down Dogwood Lane was very possibly the same man that had put Ariana in the trunk of that same car and had buried her in the forest near the now-destroyed treehouse.

There was some local gossip and speculation about the treehouse as well; Lucas overheard his mom talking with one of her friends about possible drug gangs out in the woods and the treehouse was a remnant of their workings. He had managed to keep his mouth shut about the whole thing. As far as he could tell, neither his parents nor anyone else deduced that the treehouse was actually the product of the labor of three eleven-year-old boys who just wanted a place to hang out.

Pastor Daniel finished his remarks and asked everyone to stand and sing "Amazing Grace" before they were dismissed. Lucas stood with his family and mouthed the words. Finally, the Perez family were ushered out before the rest of the attendees. The high school chorus continued to sing Amazing Grace as everyone filed out the event center and into the parking lot.

The Beaker family made their way to Bobby's charcoal Toyota Tacoma, Lucas and Allison sliding into the double cab's backseat.

"That was so sad," Stephanie Beaker said. She looked back at her children. "I pray every day that nothing happens to either of you. I just don't know what I'd do."

"We're fine, mom," Lucas said. "Nothing's going to happen to us."

"You don't know that," Allison retorted, almost rudely. She caught herself, noticing the tone with which she said that. "I'm sorry. I just can't believe she's gone." Allison looked out the window, watching the cars zipper out of the community center parking lot and into Kilgore Drive.

To lighten the mood, Bobby asked everyone what they'd like for dinner. He offered to cook on the grill and that they'd eat dinner on the patio, given the warm weather. After some consideration, they decided on grilled salmon steaks.

As they waited for their turn to leave the parking lot, talking about dinner and dessert, they never noticed the black Ford across the street, carefully concealed from the main strip behind a dilapidated 7-11 convenience store. And they certainly didn't see the man behind the car's driver seat watching the Beaker family leave the event center.

CHAPTER FIFTEEN
WEDNESDAY MARCH 19 | 9:49PM

AFTER DINNER, ALLISON retreated to her bedroom, turned on Netflix and plopped down on her bed. She pulled her phone out of the waistband of her pants and thumbed out a message to Brandon. I miss you.

She hadn't seen him since Sunday, when he came over to warn her about the note left on his windshield. Her parents, being protective and worried, had not let neither her nor Lucas out of their sight since their mom returned early from Houston.

Three bubbles came up on her phone screen, signifying a response from Brandon, but they disappeared with no message. She typed again What's wrong? and sent it.

Her phone buzzed to announce an incoming call. It

was Brandon, his face popping up on the screen. She put in her Airpods and answered. "Hello?" she said.

"Hey babe." He sounded nervous. "Listen, there's no easy way to do or say this, but…" he trailed off.

Allison knew where this was going, and she didn't like it. "You're breaking up with me? Over the phone?" She remembered to keep her voice down, but she was heated.

"I'm sorry. I just can't do this. With everything happening around us, and with what we saw. I don't know. We should have never been out that night, and I hate having to sneak around with you."

"You said you loved me just a few days ago, Brandon." Her voice was tense. "You slept with me, just the other night!"

"I know. I do love you. But we just can't do this right now. It's just too much." He apologized again.

"I guess I'll see you back at school next week," she said. "Bye." She ended the call.

Allison felt selfish. She wanted it all. She wanted the boyfriend and she wanted to be able to do what she wanted, without having to do it behind her parents' back. She wanted to have the life that she felt her friends had. Amilyn was allowed to go to San Antonio with her older sister, but she couldn't as much as walk down the park without having to announce it to the whole house.

As she thought about all this, she also understood Brandon's reasoning. It was too much, and they were both a little freaked out right now. She just didn't have anyone else to talk to about the entire ordeal. She wanted comfort and she wanted independence, and neither were within reach. She felt trapped in her head and her room.

There was a knock at her door. "Come in," she said.

The door cracked open. It was Lucas. "I was wondering if you had an extra phone charger. I think I left mine at Tyler's house."

"I think so," she got up off the bed and went to her computer desk. She pulled out the center drawer, rifling around until she found the cord. "Here you go," she said, holding it out.

He took it from her outstretched hand. "Are you okay?" he asked. "You look sad."

"Eh, I'll be fine. Just a sad day, you know?" She sat down on her computer chair. "What about you? Did you really see them put her body in the ambulance?"

Lucas sighed, and Allison felt a tinge of remorse in asking him the question. "Yeah, we did. I was with Elijah and Tyler. We were out looking -" he stopped himself.

"Looking? For what?"

Lucas sat down at the foot of his sister's bed, his feet dangling over the edge. He sank into the fullness of her comforter. "Can I tell you something?" His face was serious. It was obvious to her that Lucas was holding something in.

"You know you can trust me," she said.

"Okay, do you remember when me and Lucas and Elijah were going to build that treehouse, out in the woods?"

"Yes, of course. I drove you to Ace to buy the nails." She remembered that trip to the hardware store like it was yesterday. After school one day back in January, he had asked her to take him to buy nails and screws for a "project." When she finally coaxed the information out of him that it was a secret treehouse, she promised to keep it from their parents, as long as he ponied up thirty dollars, which he paid. What he didn't know was she had put the money back in his bedside table drawer that same evening.

"Well, we finished it last week, and we had the idea to spend the night in it. So, Friday night, we were out there." Tears welled up in his eyes. He looked away and wiped them with the sleeve of his navy-blue Henderson Lions t-shirt. He took a deep breath, holding back the tears. "We were out there, and we heard this noise outside, like someone walking through the woods. And we saw him. We saw a guy carry that body out there. And we watched him bury her."

Allison's jaw dropped; her eyes wide with disbelief.

Lucas was crying now, tears streaming down his face. She held her arms out and he hopped off the bed and embraced her.

"And now the bad guy is chasing us," he said in between sobs. "We decided to go after him, to see if we could find him to call the cops and let them know where he was. So we were riding around Monday morning when we heard the sirens. We thought maybe they'd caught him. But instead they'd found the body."

"So you think he saw you, up in the treehouse?" she asked. Lucas released her from the hug. She reached up and wiped the tears from his cheek.

"I don't know how, but yeah," he said. "And then the other night, I know that was him chasing me down the road. The police think it was just some kid playing a mean trick, but it was him. I know it."

Allison couldn't bring herself to admit to him that she knew it as well. She couldn't tell him that she, too, saw that man that same night, tossing Ariel's body into the trunk of that same black car.

She did have an idea, however.

"I believe you," she said. She stood up from the chair and put her hands on her brother's shoulders. "Tomorrow, we are going to go look for him ourselves."

119

ANDREW J BRANDT

CHAPTER SIXTEEN
THURSDAY MARCH 20 | 1:20PM

"MOM, CAN WE go to the movies? Please?" Lucas pleaded to his mother, who was working at her computer in the office.

The Beaker house was a four bedroom, with the master suite at the end of the hallway. Across from it, the Beakers converted the unused bedroom into an office, where both Stephanie and Bobby had workstations set up on opposite walls. They had ripped out the carpet, installed vinyl planking and painted the walls white. Bobby's work area, which was a wall-length drafting table, was covered in building plans and schematics. He had a television that he used as a computer monitor mounted on the wall above this. Mrs. Beaker's work area, on the other hand, was vibrant yet tidy. Beside the iMac on her wooden desk, she had a small round glass vase that held three yellow roses that her husband had harvested from the rose bush beside their front porch and an award for "2018 Realtor of the Year".

She looked up from the computer screen. "Who's we?" she inquired.

"Me and Allison," he said.

Stephanie Beaker took off her reading glasses. "I don't know if I want you guys going out by yourselves right now," she said.

"Oh, come on, mom," the boy whined. "We both have phones. We'll be fine. We just want to get out for a little bit. We've been cooped up in here for three days! I can't breathe!" Lucas grabbed at his throat with both hands and dropped to the ground, playfully writhing around while pretending to suffocate.

"Fine, fine," she relented. "But y'all come home right after the movie, please."

He popped up off the ground and hugged his mom. "Thanks mom. I love you!" He ran out of the room and into Allison's. Lucas shut the door behind him.

"She said yes," he said, beaming. "So, what's the plan?"

"Today we can just cruise around and see if we see anything suspicious." Allison pulled out her phone and opened Maps. She pinch-zoomed onto their neighborhood. Lucas leaned in to look at the screen over her shoulder. "So, we live here," she said, pointing at the lines on the screen. "Ariel lived over here. And over here," she dragged the map with her finger, "is the area of the woods where they found her. So, I say we drive around some of the neighborhoods off Kilgore and just look around."

"What do we do if we see the car?"

"We can call it in to the cops. You could even call Tyler's dad and tell him we saw the car that chased you down the other evening. They should at least send an officer over," Allison said. "They might even find Ariel's DNA in the trunk."

Lucas looked at her puzzled, and Allison realized her slip of the tongue. "How do you know he had her in the trunk?" he asked.

"Haven't you ever seen CSI? That's where they always put the body. Duh." She rolled her eyes like this was common knowledge but was relieved to brush off the question without any further interrogation.

"Well, what are we waiting for?" Lucas said. "Let's go CSI this guy!"

* * *

Lucas sat in the passenger seat of his sister's Jeep Liberty, the gray canvas seat cover tearing at the seams underneath his legs. The vehicle was a hand-me-down from their parents, who gave it to Allison when their mom bought her Lexus, and Lucas assumed that it would be his in a few years – given that the engine would hold up for five more years.

Allison had her phone plugged into the aux cable and the radio up with the rock band The Maine playing over the sound system.

"Can we stop at 7-11? I want a Slurpee," Lucas said over the music.

"Sure," she said as they pulled out onto Kilgore Drive. The main street in town, Kilgore Drive, bisected the town on the north-south axis. Nearly every business lined both sides of the street. "Keep your eyes peeled. You never know when we may see this guy."

Lucas kept his gaze out the passenger's side window, trying to take into account every vehicle in every parking lot as they drove past. None of them looked like the black Ford they were on the hunt for.

They pulled into the convenience store. On the front door of the establishment, the memorial service announcement for Ariel still hung, taped to the full glass panel. The girl's smiling face with the words "In loving memory" were printed on the poster. Allison stopped to stare at it before walking in. As many times as she'd seen Ariel at school and in volleyball practice, she now regretted never taking the time to really get to know her.

Lucas walked past her and opened the door and went straight to the Slurpee machine, pulling a bright red drink into a clear plastic cup. He shoved a red green straw into the top and took a long sip. "I haven't had one of these in forever," he said. Allison grabbed a cup for herself and poured a Dr. Pepper from the fountain.

Up at the front counter to pay for their drinks, the cashier, a hefty middle-aged Hispanic woman with long wavy black hair said, "She used to work here." She nodded her head to the memorial poster in the door. "You look to be about her age. Did you know Ariel?"

"I did. We went to school together, on the volleyball team," Allison said. "I wish I'd known her better."

"She was a sweetheart," the cashier said. "We're raising money to cover her funeral costs. Would you care to donate?"

Allison gave the cashier an extra five dollars with her payment for their soft drinks, and she and Lucas left. Driving back onto Kilgore, she told Lucas, "Pull out your phone and open Maps. Let's go drive around."

He did as she requested, and he gave her directions to the first place he thought they should go. Crossing the main road, they went over to the neighborhood where Ariel lived. Allison glanced at the parking area of the park. Feeling guilty, she looked away.

"Who would want to take her?" Lucas asked. "Like,

what kind of person would kill a teenage girl?"

"Serial killers," Allison said. "Or rapists. I don't know. There's a lot of bad people out in the world, Lucas."

Lucas continued scanning out the window. "I know. But I just want to know, what kind of person would do that. And then come after me like that in their car." He took a sip from his Slurpee. "I don't feel like he was trying to kidnap me or anything."

"Like he was just trying to scare you?" Allison asked. Given the note that was left on Brandon's car Saturday night, it made sense to her. Whoever this person was, was simply trying to scare them. But why?

"Yeah," he said. He looked at her. "He destroyed the treehouse too." He dropped his head.

"Are you serious?"

"Yeah. Me and Tyler went back out there to see if we'd left anything because we were going to call the cops, but we didn't want anyone knowing the treehouse was ours. When we got out there, it was all broken. Like he'd taken a sledgehammer to it."

"So what did y'all do?" She felt so sad for her little brother. Even though he'd kept the treehouse secret from their parents, she knew he was proud of the thing that he and his friends built.

"We ran away. We knew that he'd seen us somehow or something. And then we were too scared to go to the police."

As he was talking, blue lights flashed in the rearview mirror. "Oh no," Allison said. She pulled over to the side of the road and rolled down her window.

The officer came up to the driver's side. "Hey there. I'm Officer Sullivan with the Henderson Police Department." Allison recognized him from her conversation with him on Saturday morning. "I've stopped you because you didn't come to a complete stop at the stop sign back there."

Allison hadn't even noticed a stop sign. "I'm sorry, Officer," she said.

"Hey, you're the girl from the park last weekend, right? You had a golden retriever?" He flashed a smile.

"Yes I am. You remember?" She fished for her license in her purse.

"Of course I do. Actually, we went to school together. I graduated a couple of years ago. I was a senior when you were a freshman. Ryan Sullivan."

"Oh yeah!" Allison said, suddenly remembering him. He'd grown a little stockier since he was in high school, and probably put on another inch or two in height. They ran in different circles, but in a school as small as Henderson High, everyone was at least acquainted with everyone else.

"You played football, right?" she asked.

"Yes I did. Got a scholarship to TCU, but decided

college wasn't for me. Went to the academy and here I am. Serving and protecting."

"Well, I personally can't wait to get out of this town. I need a change of scenery," Allison said.

"I get that. And, I'm so sorry about your friend. When we were there on Saturday, we still thought it was a runaway case. Tell you what, don't worry about the license. Just be more observant, okay?" He nodded to Lucas. "Who's the little guy with you?"

Lucas waved hello. "I'm her brother."

"Well, you need to keep this young lady in line. She looks like trouble." Officer Sullivan gave Allison a wink. "Have a good day. Hope to see you again soon." He tipped his cap and went back to his car. Allison waited for him to leave before putting the Jeep in drive.

"I think he likes you," Lucas said, grinning.

"Oh whatever. Don't be weird." She gave him a playful shove.

They continued driving through the neighborhood, but none of the vehicles in the driveways or on the streets matched the description of what they were looking for. "What if he isn't even in this town any-more?" Lucas asked.

"That's a real possibility. Henderson is a small town. I couldn't imagine someone being able to hide for too long. We'll keep looking though."

Allison had definitely thought the same. After Ariel

was found and the case went from being missing person to homicide, the police presence and interest surrounding the case escalated. There was a lot of heat, and whoever it was in the black car had, Allison assumed, probably skipped down by now.

"I hope he's gone," Lucas said. "I don't want to have any more nightmares."

"I know what you mean. I don't either."

ANDREW J BRANDT

CHAPTER SEVENTEEN
THURSDAY MARCH 20 | 4:38PM

THE iPHONE BUZZED and Lucas pulled it out of his pocket. Hey bro. See if you can spend the night. It was from Tyler. The last time Lucas had seen him was on Monday, not counting the brief hello at the memorial service. Lucas typed OK and sent it.

He paused his Minecraft game on his computer and went across the hall to the home office. His dad was busy working on the plans for a building, the drawing displayed on the large television above the drafting table. Bill Withers' "Lovely Day" played on the Amazon Echo perched on the bench.

"Dad, Tyler asked if I can go over there. So, can I?"

Bobby, sitting in what was essentially a black and chrome barstool, swiveled around to see his son in the doorway. "I'll drive you over there, but I don't want you out by yourself on the bicycle right now. Give me

131

thirty minutes so I can finish this."

"Cool!" Lucas ran back into his bedroom and thumbed out I'll be there in 30 minutes and sent it.

Sweet. I've been working on something I want you to see, Tyler replied. Lucas grabbed his backpack and shoved in a pair of jeans and a Houston Astros T-shirt. He pulled on his black Chuck Taylor's and got ready to go, wondering what it was Tyler wanted to show him.

As he shut down his laptop and got all his things together, his dad knocked on the door. "Alright, I'm ready if you are," Bobby said.

The drive to Tyler's house was just a few blocks, and Bobby fiddled with the radio until he found a station that wasn't playing commercials. Lucas looked out the window and saw two little kids, no older than six, riding in circles in their driveway. Their parents sat under the covered porch watching the brother and sister. "I can't wait for everything to go back to normal so I can ride my bike again."

"I know, buddy." Bobby patted his son on the shoulder. "You'll be able to. Right now, everyone is a little on edge though."

"This is not how I wanted to spend spring break," Lucas sighed.

"Well, it's almost over. You'll be back in school on Monday."

"What do you think it's going to be like, going back?

Are they going to keep us locked down all day too?"

Bobby shot a look at his son that said knock it off. "You're not on lockdown. We just want you kids to be safe. As much as we hate to admit it, we have no idea what happened to that little girl. We don't know who took her, or why. And, as a dad, that scares me."

Lucas felt guilty. He never stopped to take into consideration how the parents must be feeling during all this. Wondering if, at any given moment, their child could or would be the next one dumped in the woods. "I'm sorry dad."

They pulled up to the curb in front of the Washington home. "It's okay, kid. I get that you're frustrated. You just have to understand and know that all we want is what's best for you. I'm not being an asshole just to be an asshole. We just want you kids to be safe." Bobby turned off the ignition. "I'm gonna say hi to John while we're here."

They went up to the front door and rang the doorbell. Victoria, dressed in her workout attire, leggings and a light pink Lululemon tank top answered, "Hey y'all, come on in! Tyler's been so antsy, wanting you boys to come over again."

Bobby and Lucas entered the home, and John came in from the garage to greet them as well. The two men went back out to the garage, talking about Mr. Washington's latest restoration project.

Lucas went to Tyler's bedroom, where Tyler and Elijah were playing Fortnite. "Hey guys!" Lucas fist-bumped both of them. "I'm so glad we're all here again. I've felt like a prisoner!"

Elijah, not looking away from the television while controlling his character through the virtual brush and looking for an enemy, "Oh, dude. Same. I practically had to beg my mom to let me come over here."

"So, what did you want to show me?" Lucas asked Tyler.

"I'll pull it out in a second, but I want to wait til later this evening before doing anything. But let's just say, we've got some work to do," Tyler said with a grin.

Elijah's character popped up out of the brush on the screen and shot the other player on the screen. The words "Victory Royale #1" popped up and his character danced to the victory music. "Finally!" Elijah exclaimed. "I've been going after that dude for twenty minutes!"

Bobby popped his head in the bedroom door. "Hey kid, I'm leaving. Be good for John and Vic." Lucas hugged his dad goodbye and the man left. The boys watched the Toyota Tacoma drive off, back toward the Beaker home.

"I was really hoping they'd let you ride your bike over," Tyler said, turning to Lucas.

"So do I. But they don't want me out on it by myself

right now. That's why my dad drove me over," Lucas said.

Elijah sat down the Xbox controller and said, "That sucks. We could have definitely used it for tonight."

Lucas looked at his friends, confused. "Why? What's happening tonight?"

CHAPTER EIGHTEEN
THURSDAY MARCH 20 | 6:52PM

TYLER REACHED INTO the top drawer of the wooden nightstand beside his bed and pulled out a sheet of paper. He handed it, still folded, to Lucas. Lucas unfolded it and pursed his lips, unsure of what he was reading. It was a computer printout with addresses and vehicle types with license plate numbers. Five of the listings were circled with black pen. "What is this?" he asked.

"Long story short, my dad has this program at work that lets you do a database search for the whole county. You can search for vehicle registrations, vehicle types, and stuff like that."

Lucas looked up from the paper at Tyler, who, by judging the look on his face, was very proud of himself.

He couldn't believe they had access to this type of information.

"Last night, after he and my mom went to bed, I got on the computer and started doing some investigating. I was able to log in to the database program. That," he said, confidently, "is a list of every black Ford vehicle registered in the county. The ones circled are the ones that aren't pickups or SUVs." He pointed at the circled items on the list. "Our guy is on here. And we're going to find him."

Lucas read each listing individually across the page, the crease from the fold in between the "vehicle type" and "address" columns. As he scanned the page, he saw things like Ford Excursion and F250 crossed off. Ford Fusion, Ford Fiesta and Taurus were circled. One of these, they assumed, was the suspect's possible vehicle.

"I can't believe you were able to do this!" Lucas hadn't been this elated since before the treehouse was completed. This was more than just aimlessly running around town hoping to see the black car. This was actual progress, a plan that had action. As he scanned the page, however, he noticed something missing. "Where are the names? It just lists addresses and license plates."

"Apparently you have to put in another password to access some more confidential data, and I couldn't figure that one out. But this has everything we need,"

Tyler said. "All we have to do now is find the car."

Lucas nodded in agreement. The names of the people on the list weren't as necessary as simply finding the vehicle. Once they found the vehicle, they knew they had the killer. "Where are these addresses in town?" Lucas asked.

Elijah pulled a black Dell Chromebook from his backpack and opened it up. "I've already mapped them out," he said as the Google maps page loaded. "Tyler told me when I got here, so I started working on this. As you can see here," he pointed at the screen where he'd created a route that connected each address on the list, "we can start here, at Tyler's, and go south before coming back up on the other side of Kilgore."

"Since you your parents wouldn't let you bring your bike, you can ride on my pegs. Which may be best. That way you can focus on the cars at these addresses without having to ride as well. But tonight, after my parents go to bed, we're going out there and finding this guy," Tyler said.

Lucas liked the plan, as dangerous as it sounded. Aside from getting caught sneaking out, there was also the risk of being seen by the guy. "So, I just have to identify the car that tried to run me over?"

"Yup," Tyler affirmed. "That's all we have to do. On this list, find the one that tried to run you over. If you can do that, we can take that information to the cops. They'll arrest him for what he did to you, and then they'll find that girl's DNA in the car some-where."

"Right," Elijah said. "If he drove her body out to the woods in that same car, they'd be able to find her DNA in it. We could literally get this case solved to-night. Do you think you'd recognize the car again if you saw it?"

Lucas thought for a second. "I think so, yeah. I'd need to see the front end. I don't think I could ever forget those headlights though. When I thought he was going to run me over, they were right on me. Wait a second…"

"What?" Tyler asked.

"I just remembered. I rode my bike over the curb and hid in the bushes on the side of a house over there. When he drove off, I noticed that one of the back lights was broken and taped over.

"That's awesome!" Elijah said. "That's the clue we need!"

Tyler fist bumped Lucas. "We're definitely going to get this guy."

Elijah went back to the computer screen. "I'm go-ing to send this map to my phone. When we leave to-night, I'll navigate. Tyler will give you a pump and you look for the car with the broken tail light."

Lucas was beaming. For the first time in almost a

week, he wasn't scared, and he could tell his friends were feeling the same way. He was excited and nervously impatient. "What time do we head out?"

"My parents usually go to bed around eleven on the weekends. I think sometime after that, we should be fine," Tyler said.

Mrs. Washington called for them from the kitchen, "Dinner's ready, boys!"

Tyler took the paper, folded it up and put it in the back pocket of his Old Navy jeans. "Let's go eat. We're gonna need our energy for tonight."

ANDREW J BRANDT

CHAPTER NINETEEN
THURSDAY MARCH 20 | 9:10PM

"OH MY GOD!" Allison squealed and wrapped her arms around Amilyn. "It feels like it's been forever!" Amilyn had popped into her room, almost appearing from thin air in the doorway. She was in a short denim skirt and maroon shirt that hugged her curves with Texas A&M emblazoned across her chest.

"I know! I'm pretty sure my parents tracked my phone the whole time I drove over. They almost didn't let me come over, but I told them I was getting cabin fever."

Allison released her friend from her grasp. They shut the bedroom door and plopped on the bed. "It's been so crazy here," Allison said. "Like, I never thought anything like this could happen in Henderson."

143

"I know. My parents have been hovering like crazy!" Amilyn said. "They want to know where I am every second of the day. Literally, my dad followed me to work yesterday to make sure I got there safe."

"My parents actually let Lucas and me go out yesterday afternoon. This whole thing has hit him pretty hard."

"I'm sure it's scarier for the little kids," Amilyn said, but Allison knew why the situation had Lucas freaked out, and it didn't have anything to do with his age.

"So, listen," Amilyn said, bringing her voice down. "You know Jeremy, from the football team, right?"

Allison knew exactly who she was talking about, and she was definitely not a fan. Jeremy Collins was a jock and a jerk of the highest order. He was the kind of boy who thought the number of pounds on the bench press made up for the lack of cells in his brain.

"Yeah, why?" she asked, the disgust in her voice not disguised in the least.

"Well, he's having a party tonight at his place. Everyone is going. There's going to be a lot of cute boys there."

"I don't know, Am. The last thing I want is boys."

"I understand. Well, let's at least go and have a good time. Pretty much everyone from the volleyball team will be there."

Allison didn't want to let her friend down or seem

like a loser, but the last thing she wanted to do was be around a bunch of drunk kids. "Can we just hang out here, Am? It's been a crazy week."

"It has been a crazy week, so let's go out and get drunk and forget about it!"

A week ago, Allison would have been all about it. But now, after what she'd witnessed, and watching her little brother break down with what he and his friends had seen, she simply didn't have any interest in doing anything stupid.

"Can you imagine how freaked out my parents would be if they saw that we were gone? They'd think the worst. I mean, Ari died last Friday, and everyone thought she had just run away. Now, our parents would worry if we're dead."

"Don't be so dramatic, Allison." Amilyn said.

"I'm not being dramatic!" Allison could feel the heat rising in her face. "Ari was murdered and whoever did it is still out there. You can go, but I'm not. Besides, I thought you came over here to hang out with me."

Amilyn stood up. "I do want to hang out with you, but I told some of the other girls I'd go to the party. If I go just for a little bit, can I leave my phone here? My parents track my location."

"Fine," Allison relented, feeling that her burst of frustration was in the wrong. "But please don't do anything stupid."

"I won't, I promise. Also, hide my phone so your mom doesn't see it or anything." Amilyn handed Allison the red iPhone and Allison shoved it in the pocket of her shorts. Amilyn hugged Allison. "Promise you'll be right back?"

"I promise. I'm just going to make an appearance and I'll come right back." Allison opened the door for her.

Mrs. Beaker was in the hallway, coming out of her office. "Are you leaving already?"

"Oh, she'll be right back, mom," Allison said, shooting a glance at her friend. "She forgot some stuff at home."

"Yeah, I'll be back in about thirty minutes, if that's alright."

"Of course, sweetie. Just drive safely."

Amilyn waved goodbye.

* * *

It had been over two hours, and Amilyn still wasn't back. Allison would have been worried, but according to the Snapchat stories from everyone out at Jeremy's party, she was having a great time. Allison felt a touch of regret, but more than anything she was upset that her friend left her high and dry and basically used her as an alibi so she could go party.

It was things like this that made her want to go to college far away. She wanted to start over, with new friends and new experiences without any preconceived notions about who she was.

There was a knock at her door. "Come in," she said.

It was her mother, dressed for bed. "Is your friend not coming back?"

"Oh, no." Allison looked at the time on her phone. It was almost midnight. "She said she was having cramps."

"Oh, poor girl. I don't miss those days. Well, I'm off to bed. Goodnight, sweetie."

"Goodnight, mom."

As her mom shut the door, Allison sat up. "Wait, mom?"

The woman opened it. "Yes?"

"I just wanted to tell you I love you."

Her mother beamed. "I love you too, sweetie. I think you're a wonderful young lady. I'll see you in the morning."

She shut the door and Allison laid back down. Her phone dinged. She hoped it was from Amilyn, letting her know she was on her way back. She unlocked the screen. It was not from her friend. Instead she opened it to see a text message from Brandon.

Hey are you still awake?

Yes, she replied

Can we talk?

About?

Us. Unlock your window. I want to come over. Just talk.

Allison paused for a moment, deciding what she wanted to do. A part of her wanted to tell him to piss off. But at the same time, she really wanted closure on their relationship. She had no desire to continue hiding or sneaking around, and she wanted to be able to tell him this. She wanted to tell him she had no desire to go to Stephen F. Austin University with him, and that she was getting away from this town for good.

NO SEX.

No sex, he replied.

OK.

I'll be there in about 30 min.

Allison went to the window Brandon usually came in through and lifted the latches. She then laid back on her bed to scroll through her newsfeeds. Waiting for Brandon, her eyelids began to feel heavy and she closed them to rest for a few minutes.

CHAPTER TWENTY
THURSDAY MARCH 20 | 11:25PM

TYLER CAREFULLY LIFTED the glass pane window. At nearly midnight, the air blowing in had cooled off to a chill. Earlier in the day, Tyler had popped the screen out of its bracket so he and his friends would be able to sneak out efficiently. He lifted himself out through the window sill and dropped to the ground outside, landing on his feet and crouching. "Okay," he whispered to his friends staring out the open hole into the night. "We're good."

Lucas followed, with Elijah coming out last and he shut the window on his way out, leaving a half-inch crack so they could lift it back up easily when they returned from their investigation.

They ran around the backside of the house, ducking under the other windows as they passed them, where

Tyler and Elijah had placed their bicycles earlier in the day. Lucas hopped on the back pegs of Tyler's bike and they rode out into the street, heading south toward the first house on the database list.

The first stop was off Marshall Street, which was less than half a mile from Tyler's house. The cool night air blew on blew on their faces and made Lucas's nose burn as they rode along. He wrapped his hands in the sleeves of his black Nike hoodie so that they'd stay warm while holding on to Tyler's shoulders. As the boys rode, they avoided the main streets and checked for any sign of oncoming traffic before crossing inter-sections.

"Turn left up here," Elijah said, his phone mounted to his handlebars of his bicycle and navigating them through the dark streets.

Tyler turned at the intersection, the green street sign reading "Marshall" under the illumination of a high street lamp.

"The address is 1107, up on the left," Elijah called out again. This part of the street was incredibly dark with the only light coming from the porch lights that were left on. The sidewalks were cracked and many of the yards were unkempt, the only vegetation growing were weeds instead of manicured grass.

1107 Marshall was a house of white siding, with several panels chipping paint. The driveway was not paved but made up of large flat stones set in the dirt. The front yard was enclosed in a chain-link fence.

The boys rode up to the curb and hid behind a tree, its branches bare, not having yet grown leaves from its winter hibernation.

In the driveway was a black Ford Fiesta. Lucas hopped off Tyler's bicycle pegs and snuck up to the rear fender, keeping out of the light from the porch. He checked the rear passenger tail light. It was intact.

Lucas jogged back to his friends, who were still crouched near the naked tree. "Not this one, but this neighborhood creeps me out. Let's go."

They mounted the bicycles and turned back toward the direction they came from, turning back to the north at the intersection. "Where to next, Elijah?" Tyler asked.

Elijah manipulated his phone attached to his handlebars. "We need to cross Evenside, toward Katy Drive," he said.

Lucas held on to Tyler's shoulders over the bumps in the road as they crossed Evenside Drive, looking for any sign of life on the streets. So far, they seemed to be the only people out and awake. Occasionally a dog would bark from the backyard of a house, but other than that, the streets at night were eerily quiet.

Lucas was so used to the ambient sounds during the day that these same streets and neighborhoods that he saw on a daily basis were alien to him now.

They turned onto Katy Drive, with Elijah leading the way and they approached the next house on the list. 2112 Katy Drive was an orange brick cottage with a large porch wrapped around the front of the house. A child's tricycle lay on its side beside the front steps of the porch. In the driveway, there were two vehicles, a Ford Taurus and a navy blue GMC Acadia.

Again, like last time, Lucas hopped off the back of Tyler's bicycle and approached the Taurus. With one look at the rear fender, he turned back. "Strike two," he said. "It's not this one either. Where's the next one?"

"Larkwood Street," Elijah said.

"That's pretty far," Tyler said.

"It's about a mile, close to the edge of the woods. But the next two are on the way back to your house from there."

Tyler looked at the Timex on his wrist and illuminated the watch face. "It's just after midnight," he said. We need to hurry. The longer we're out, the more we're at risk of getting caught or being seen."

They pedaled back east toward the place where the woods bumped against the neighborhoods, using the canopy of the forest outcropping as camouflage and cover.

After about ten minutes of riding, they reached

Larkwood Street. The houses were big and the opposite of the dilapidated homes that they'd seen on Marshall. Some of the residences were two-story with nicely manicured lawns.

"Are you sure we're in the right place?" Lucas asked.

"I think so," Tyler said. "It's on the list."

"Which address?" Lucas asked Elijah, who continued to ride slightly ahead of them.

"3402, up ahead on the right," he said.

They passed a couple of houses and advanced to the house on the list. Even in the dark, it was gorgeous. Shrubs lined the front of the house beneath the windows. The front porch was framed with round white columns and the brick looked polished and clean.

There were no vehicles in the driveway.

"Guys, what do we do?" Elijah asked.

Offset from the front of the house, the driveway extended toward the back of the residence, with a two car garage detached from the home. Lucas stepped off the pegs. "I'm going to look in the garage," he said defiantly.

"I don't know man, this doesn't feel right," Tyler said. "This one may be on the list by mistake."

"Maybe we should just go on to the next one," Elijah said.

"No way, guys. We won't know for sure unless we

look in that garage," Lucas said.

Slowly, crouching down and staying out of the swath of light illuminating the front porch of the house, Lucas crept up to the garage. It was a double bay garage with separate doors for each entrance. Each roll-up door had a row of windows about two-thirds of the way up, which was just above Lucas's head.

He ran back toward his friends, who had pulled their bicycles behind a row of shrubs lining the house next door and were crouching in the branches. Lucas knelt down with them. "The windows are too high. I can't see in," he said. "I need one of you to come with me and lift me up."

"I'll do it," Tyler said. He turned to Elijah. "Keep your eyes peeled. Cover us."

Tyler and Lucas approached the garage. Lucas's heart raced. They got to the garage doors and Tyler laced his fingers to form a step for Lucas. Tyler hoisted his friend up and Lucas grabbed onto the window sills with the tips of his fingers to pull himself up so he could see in.

It was dark in the garage, but he could make out the outline of a little black Ford. With his left hand, he grabbed his iPhone and turned on the flashlight.

"What the hell are you doing?" Tyler said, his voice strained. He shifted his weight to better hold Lucas.

"I'm trying to see," Lucas said.

"Elijah should have done this. He's heavier than me."

"Yeah," Lucas retorted, "but you're taller."

Lucas peered in, the flashlight on the back of his phone illuminating the space so that he could see in. The words "Five Hundred" were embossed in a silver emblem on the trunk of the car. Lucas almost lost his balance when he gasped at what he saw. The passenger tail light was broken, with strips of red tape covering the hole.

"Holy shit, dude." Lucas looked down at Tyler. "That's the car."

.

.

CHAPTER TWENTY ONE
FRIDAY MARCH 21 | 12:10AM

"ARE YOU SURE?" Tyler asked, his voice still strained from holding Lucas on his shoulders.

Lucas asked to be let down and Tyler did so more than willingly. "Definitely sure. Red tape and everything. This is the car." Lucas's eyes were wide with both excitement and terror.

Lucas's phone buzzed in his pocket. He pulled it out to see a text message from Elijah, who was still in the shrubs keeping a lookout for them. The message read *911*. Lucas looked up at Tyler and they both bolted as quietly as possible back to Elijah's hiding spot.

"I saw someone in the house, through the window," Elijah whispered.

"Well, this is definitely the house," Lucas said. "The car is in the garage."

"Check it out," Elijah said, pointing toward a window facing them. A light was on, and there was definitely movement in the house, though it was obscured through the miniblinds. They watched for a couple of minutes but were unable to make out what was happening.

Then, the light shut off. "Maybe he was going to the bathroom or something," Lucas whispered.

The sound of the garage door opening startled them. Elijah nearly jumped out of the bushes and Tyler grabbed him. The tail lights winked to signify the car being unlocked remotely. From a back door, out of sight from their perch, a man walked into the garage and got in the car. He turned it on, and reversed it out of the driveway, the driver's side door passing not even two meters from where they were hiding.

The garage door shut automatically, the car backed into the street, turned left and drove off.

"What are we doing?" Tyler said. "We gotta go after him!"

They jumped out of the shrubs, pulled the bicycles upright and rode off in the same direction the car went. The Ford's driving lights were dark, but they could still see the vehicle as it passed under the street lamps that lined Larkwood Drive. Lucas could feel Tyler pumping his legs on the pedals, his body swaying as he shifted his weight.

"We can't get too close. Don't want him to see us," Tyler said over his shoulder.

"Just don't lose him," Lucas said. "Look he's turning again!" He pointed ahead of them.

"I see it!" Tyler responded.

Elijah called out, "He's heading back toward Kilgore!"

They continued riding, pounding the pedals as hard as they could. As they crossed Kilgore Drive, the lights above the main city strip were much brighter, which Lucas knew meant they could be seen just as easily as a vehicle. Three boys out on bicycles at this time of night would get attention more than a vehicle driving along the same stretch of road.

"Where do you think he's going?" Lucas asked.

Tyler, breathless but continuing to ride as hard as he could, said, "I don't know, but we've got to stay with him."

Elijah, riding beside them said, "If he's out kidnapping someone else, we can get the cops there immediately!"

They watched as the car turned right off of Kilgore. They chased him, still tailing by about two blocks' distance. Lucas realized they were getting close to their neighborhood.

The car turned again, left this time. The boys turned

onto the same street, Bismarck Lane. The car had disappeared. "Where did he go?" Elijah asked, perplexed.

Tyler rode a little further up to the next block and looked down both north and south of the intersection. They had lost him.

"Damnit!" Tyler exclaimed.

"Look, we know where he lives now," Elijah said, pulling up beside Lucas and Tyler them on his bike. "We can still go back to the old plan and call the cops in the morning. Now we know for sure though. This is our guy."

"But why was he out here tonight?" Tyler said, exacerbated. "And how did we lose him?"

"It's okay, Tyler," Lucas said. "Let's go back home. In the morning, we can call it in." He hopped off the pegs. "Let me pedal and you ride. You've got no gas."

Tyler swung his leg around off the seat and handed the handlebars to Lucas. Lucas mounted the bike and Tyler climbed onto the pegs. They had ridden nearly five miles at this point, and with the extra weight of Lucas riding on the back, Tyler was exhausted.

They took it easy riding back to Tyler's house; not necessarily taking their time but at the same time not going all out to get there as quickly as possible. Dogwood Lane intersected Bismarck, and they were only six blocks from Tyler's house. Lucas's house was on the corner two blocks away. "Take it slow up here, Elijah," Lucas said. "My parents have cameras facing the street."

They crossed to the far side of the street and passed Lucas's house. Lucas looked at the house and nearly crashed the bicycle. There, the black car was parked two houses down, and Allison was being led into the backseat. As her head disappeared into the vehicle, she turned, and they momentarily made eye contact. Lucas and his friends sat frozen in the middle of Dogwood Lane watching. The man in the car threw something into the lawn across the street from where he'd parked, got in the car, and drove off.

ANDREW J BRANDT

CHAPTER TWENTY TWO
FRIDAY MARCH 21 | 12:25AM

ALLISON WAS STARTLED awake by the buzzing of her phone. She looked at the time. 12:25am. She opened the text message; it was from Brandon, which meant he was close. *Come to the window.*

She went to the window. The phone buzzed again. *Open it.*

She was confused but opened the window. Again, a buzz. *Climb out.*

She hesitated. Something felt off. Allison considered shutting it. The phone buzzed. This time, it was a call instead of a text. Brandon's face filled the screen.

"Hello?"

"Listen to me right now." The voice on the other end was not Brandon's. It was a man's voice, older and almost monotone. "Do not hang up. Your name is Allison Hanes. Your mother is Stephanie Beaker. Your stepfather is Bobby Beaker. Your little brother, Lucas Beaker, is eleven years old. He is in the sixth grade at Henderson Middle School. Do everything I say, and you and your family will be fine. I will not hurt you. But if you do not follow my instructions to the letter, I will kill your little brother and your parents."

Fear immediately welled up in her. She felt her stomach sink. The voice continued. "Now, listen closely. After I hang up with you, climb out the window, and walk two houses to your right. Bring your phone. There is a black Ford. I will open the door for you. Get in the backseat. Again, do not make me hurt your family." The voice was calm and smooth. The tone and the words were juxtaposed, as the threats did not match the sound.

Allison, in shock, did as the voice said. Clutching her phone in her hand, she crawled out the window. She was cold and wished she'd grabbed a sweater, but she was already outside and didn't know what would happen if she made any sudden movements or deviated from her instructions.

She could see the car, its lights completely dark. As she approached, a man appeared from the driver's seat and opened the rear door on the driver's side. He was large, both tall and stocky. He was dressed in a black button up and dark jeans. Black wayfarer glasses framed his eyes, light brown and soft like caramel. Despite his size, he looked kind, like a young college professor.

"Your phone, please," he requested with his hand outstretched. Allison handed it to him, and he threw it across the street, the device landing with a bounce in one of her neighbors' yards.

Like an Uber from a nightmare, she got in the car. Something out of the corner of her eye caught her attention. Some light or reflection glinted, and she looked down Dogwood Lane. She must have been hallucinating, she thought, because Allison would swear that she saw her brother and his two friends, no more than a hundred yards away, staring at her.

"I know you're really scared right now," the driver said as he put the vehicle in drive and accelerated south on Dogwood Lane. "But I promise you, you'll be fine. I'm not going to hurt you."

Allison was speechless. A million thoughts zoomed through her brain, but she couldn't focus to form a cognitive understanding of what was truly going on.

The driver, her abductor, looked at her through the rearview mirror with those soft caramel eyes. "Don't be frightened, okay? You're going to be fine. I'm not going to hurt you," he repeated. The way he said it, his voice smooth and caring, made Allison almost believe it.

She didn't say a word, but simply looked out the window. She was amazed and perplexed. He didn't tape her up, didn't bind her hands. She could easily reach over the driver's seat and strangle the man right here. He would crash the car and she could make a run for it. At a stop sign, she gently tested the door handle. The child safety lock was engaged; she couldn't open it.

But, if she did try to strangle him, she thought, she could also end up injured or worse. There didn't seem to be an easy way out of this at the moment. More importantly, her family was safe, at least for the time being. If this man kept his word, they would be left unharmed.

The man in the driver's seat wasn't big or even very intimidating. A man, most likely in his early to mid-thirties of average height and weight, with a few specks of gray coming through the part and sides in his dark walnut hair   , who seemed more destined for a law firm than a kidnapping.

He looked at her again through the rearview. "What kind of music do you like? I want you to feel comfortable."

He pushed the radio dial and scanned the FM channels until an Imagine Dragons song piped through the stereo system. "This okay?" he asked. Allison didn't respond. She simply watched the houses pass as they drove. She recognized a few of them, but in the darkness, she didn't know which direction they were heading.

"Where are you taking me?" she finally spoke.

"To my safehouse. The buyer will be arriving in a few hours."

"The buyer?"

"I'll tell you more when we get there."

"So, you're not going to kill me?"

His eyes darted to her through the mirror again. "My god, no. I know, some of the things I said earlier sounded scary. But I promise you, you're fine. No one is getting killed tonight. I'm so sorry that I have to do this to you."

She was confused by his answer, and his apology. She didn't understand what any of it meant. This was the same guy, supposedly, that killed Ariana a week earlier. How could he tell her she was safe, in such a gentle and tender fashion? How could he threaten to kill her family in the same voice that he asked her what music she liked?

The car pulled into an apartment complex, which Allison knew was on the far south side of Henderson. He drove around one of the buildings and pulled into an open garage door attached the bottom level of a townhouse. The garage door shut behind them as he put the vehicle in park, and he disengaged the ignition.

They sat in the dark until the garage door was fully closed.

He got out of the car and opened the door for her. "Get out slowly and keep your hands in view. I don't want to bind you and I don't want to hurt you, so don't make me," he said.

She did as he instructed, keeping her hands up and over her head. She felt like a prisoner. She was a prisoner. "Now walk, to the door. Stop at the door and I will open it for you."

Allison walked to the door that led into the apartment. As she stood in front of it, the man reached around her to open it. The door led into the kitchen of the apartment. It was clean and bright, with stainless steel appliances and beautiful marble countertops.

"Walk to your left," he instructed. "There is a door on the right. I will open it for you."

She walked to it, he opened it, and she looked into a bedroom. It was bare except for a twin bed with a white comforter and solitary pillow in a matching white pillowcase. The carpet was a dark navy. "This is yours for the rest of the night."

"What is happening?" she asked.

"You're being sold," he said.

"To who?"

"A buyer."

"But, why?" The pit in her stomach was heavy. She

could feel panic coming in.

"Sit down on the bed," he said. She hesitated. "I said sit." He was more forceful with his tone and she followed his instruction.

"Thank you. I don't want to be angry." He stood in the doorway.

"Why did you kill her? Why did you kill Ari?" Tears started to flow down her cheeks. She wondered if that same fate was coming for her, despite this man's calm demeanor.

He looked down at the floor and sighed. His arms crossed in front of his chest. When he looked back up at her, his eyes were full of genuine sadness. "That," he said with a pause, "was an accident."

"What do you mean? I saw you put her body in your trunk."

"I know. It started out easily, just like with you. But she tried to run, and when she did, she slipped and hit her head on the concrete. She had a seizure. And then," he shook his head, "she was gone."

"So why dump her in the woods?" Allison said.

"I didn't know what else to do. But my buyer is expecting a teenage girl, and I have to provide one." "I don't understand."

"I know you don't, and I know it's a lot of information to process. I'm so glad you followed my instructions, though. This will be very easy for you." He stepped toward her and she tensed up. "It's okay. Like I said, I'm not going to hurt you."

He crouched down in front of her, still sitting on the edge of the bed, and he took her hand. "You're beautiful. I'm so sorry I have to do this. I know you're scared, and I wish I could make you not be."

"Why are you doing this?"

He looked at her with those caramel eyes. "Because this is how I take care of my family."

CHAPTER TWENTY THREE
FRIDAY MARCH 21 | 12:30AM

"HE TOOK HER!" Lucas screamed. His voice, shrill and pitchy, echoed through the neighborhood.

Tyler and Elijah stood slack jawed next to Lucas in the middle of the street as the car drove away, its taillights, dimming as it disappeared in the night.

Lucas jumped off the back of Tyler's bicycle and ran toward the spot where the car had been parked. The man had thrown something into the yard of the house across the street. Searching through the grass of the neighbor's lawn, he found it. It was Allison's phone, face down in the yard with dirt and grass clippings sticking to the case. The screen had a crack diagonally down its face.

He picked it up and held it in the air. "It's her phone!" he said as he ran back to his friends, still standing in the street. Several times in the past, he had seen her use the lock code to unlock it, and it was a pattern that he hoped he could replicate. He tried it, carefully pressing 1-3-4-6-7-9, and the screen opened for him. "We're in!"

"Let's get out of the middle of the street, bro," Tyler said. Rolling the bicycles beside them, they ran across the street into Lucas's front yard.

Tyler and Elijah huddled over Lucas's shoulders as he opened up her text messages. The most recent ones were from Brandon.

"Isn't that your sister's boyfriend?" Elijah asked.

Lucas nodded as he read the messages. He then opened the most recent calls. The call log showed Brandon's as the last number to call her.

"Bro. I think your sister's boyfriend is a serial killer!" Tyler said.

Lucas checked the time stamp on the phone call and then on the text messages. Brandon had told her he was coming over, and then he called her. After which, Allison got in the car with him. The same car that tried to run him over. He couldn't believe it.

The light on the front porch of Lucas's house turned on and the front door swung open. Bobby Beaker stood in the doorway in a pair of gray Nike sweatpants and a Houston Astros t-shirt. "What the hell are you boys doing out here?" he asked with a voice full of irritation and sleep.

"Dad!" Lucas exclaimed, holding Allison's phone in the air. "Brandon took Allison!"

Lucas ran up to the porch and both Tyler and Elijah followed, dumping their bikes in the grass. Bobby Beaker stood in the open glass pane door and Lucas wrapped his arms around the man's waist.

"Dad, we know who killed that girl in the woods. And now Allison is in trouble." Bobby held his son and tried to calculate in his head what the boy had just told him.

"What are you talking about, son? C'mon, let's go inside." He waved at Lucas and Elijah. "You boys get in here."

They walked in the house and Bobby turned on the light in the dining room. All three boys surrounded the man and tried talking all at once. "Hold up, hold up," Bobby said, calming them down. "I can't understand what you're saying. One at time. Now what is going on?"

"Dad, we know who killed that girl, out in the woods. It was the same guy that tried to run me over. And, we just saw him take Allison. It was her boyfriend. Look," Lucas handed his dad the phone. "The text messages."

Bobby read the messages on the device and the color ran from his face. He dropped the phone on the table and ran back to Allison's bedroom, where he found the bedroom window was still open.

"Stephanie!" he called out into the hallway. "Wake up, Allison's gone!"

Bobby ran back into the dining room, where Lucas and his friends sat at the table. He had his cell phone in his hand and he dialed 911. "Yes, my name is Bobby Beaker. I'm at 3612 Locust Dr. My daughter was just abducted from her bedroom. We believe it was her boyfriend."

After a few seconds, he hung up the call. He turned to the boys and rested his hands on the back of the chair at the head of the table. "Okay, I need you to tell me everything."

CHAPTER TWENTY FOUR
FRIDAY MARCH 21 | 12:52AM

"I DON'T GET it. What do you mean, take care of your family?"

"This is how I make money. I have three sons. My youngest has a heart defect. My wife lost her job about a year ago, and we lost insurance. This is how I take care of them. I sell young women, like you, to buyers from Mexico."

"I'm going to Mexico?"

"Just for a little while. You're sixteen, so you'll age out in a couple of years. The men there that buy girls like them young. As long as you're good and don't make any trouble, you'll be released, and you will be able to eventually find yourself back home."

She began sobbing again. "You called me from Brandon's phone. Is he in on this too? Is that why he was with me?"

"Oh, no, not at all." He stood up and pulled a tissue from his pocket. "Here," he said handing it to her.

She took it from his hand and pressed it against her eyes, soaking the tissue with tears.

He continued, "No, your boyfriend is unaware of your current situation. Or, ex-boyfriend, if I read the messages between you correctly. You wouldn't believe how easy it is to clone a cell phone's SIM card."

She looked at him, bewildered. "Clone?"

"Yes. It's very simple. I saw you two across the street from the park last week. I followed you and him the next day, to see if you were a threat. I followed him to his house. I was able to cross-reference his address with the billing system at," he paused, not wanting to tell her the exact place, "the cell phone store. Once I had that, I looked up the account information. I saw which number on the account showed the most activity congruent to a teenager's usage and cloned his SIM card."

"So, you sent the messages? Not Brandon?"

"Nope. As far as I know, Brandon has moved on from you. Looking through the messages he's been sending lately, he seems to really have a thing for your friend." He pulled out his cell phone and scrolled through the screen. "Amilyn? That name mean anything to you?"

Allison felt the sting in her chest. That must have

been why Amilyn never showed back up tonight. She and Brandon were hooking up at that party, leaving her waiting and wondering. She felt used and tossed aside. Her best friend and now ex-boyfriend left her and now she was this man's hostage.

"I can't believe this. How? How did you even see us at the park?"

"How did I see you? Well, that car of his isn't exactly inconspicuous. Teenagers," he said with a huff. "You all have to show off all the time. There's nothing subtle about being a teenager. In fact, I bet he and your friend are enjoying themselves right now in the same backseat that you and he did last week."

"Please stop. I don't want to hear about it." She sobbed. Changing the subject, she asked, "What about my brother? Why did you try to run him over? He didn't do anything to you."

"I wasn't actually going to hit him," he said, leaning into the doorframe and crossing his arms. "He and his little friends were getting too curious. I needed to scare him off. I thought if I could put the fear of God into him, he'd not dabble in little boy spy fantasies, trying to find the man in the woods. You know how boys can be."

Allison couldn't stop the tears from flowing down her face. She could not believe she was in this situation. And now, faced with the idea of being sold into sex slavery, she could barely keep it together.

"Don't cry, Allison," the man said. "I know this is a lot right now, but you're not going to die. To be honest, I was scared when I got into this business."

"Yeah, but you're not the one being sold." It was getting late and her eyes were feeling heavy from crying and lack of sleep.

The man, standing in the doorway, shook his head and said, "You're right. But I also can't stop. I'm in this longer than you are. You'll be out of the market in two years, tops. Me? If I don't give them what they want, they come after me. There's no out for me. But, my son is still alive because of this. Because of your small sacrifice, a little boy gets to live."

"But surely you can get out! Just leave!" she was almost pleading at this point. "Take your family to some other city."

He shook his head. "It's not that easy. Besides, why do you think we're in Henderson? No one is going to pay attention to a couple of missing girls from a tiny Texas town. There's some heat now but it will die down, and we will move on to the next town."

He looked at the watch on his wrist. "They'll be here in about an hour. You'll be able to get some sleep on the drive to Houston."

She felt some fullness in her bladder. Now that the adrenaline and initial fear had somewhat subsided, she could tell she really needed to go. "I need to use the bathroom," she said, her nose full of snot and tears staining her cheeks.

"Okay. Stand up and place your hands above your head." Allison stood up from the bed, her knees shaking from shock and lifted her arms.

"Keep your hands up and walk toward me." She did as instructed, taking the five steps to the man standing in the doorframe. "I'm going to lead you to the bathroom. There are bars on the window, so don't even try to get out. Like I said, I do not want to hurt you."

He grabbed her by the arm and led her down the short hallway to the bathroom. It was impossibly small, with a sink, toilet and stand-up shower cramped in a space not much bigger than a closet. The open door nearly grazed across the side of the white porcelain sink as it opened. "Can I trust you?" he asked her.

"Yes," she said sheepishly.

"Good. I will close the door and give you sixty seconds. After that, the door will open. Understand?"

Allison nodded yes. He let her go, and she walked into the bathroom. The man shut the door behind her. She went to the toilet and pulled her shorts down. She felt something in the pocket.

It was Amilyn's phone.

A feeling of joy and elation ran through her body like lightning. She had forgotten that she'd stuck the phone in her pocket when Amilyn left for the party. She wanted to scream and shout in this little piece of providence, but she knew she had to be quiet. She also knew she couldn't make a phone call, but she had an idea.

Thumbing at the screen, she input the lock code—Amilyn's birthday—and the phone opened up for her. In the text messages, she typed in Lucas's phone number, and hit "Share my location". She then wrapped the phone in toilet paper and shoved it into the trash can beside the toilet.

The bathroom door swung open as she pulled her shorts back up. The man stood in the door. "Time's up," he said.

She flushed the toilet, never having had a chance to actually relieve her bladder. With a slight smile forming at the corners of her mouth she said, "I feel much better now."

CHAPTER TWENTY FIVE
FRIDAY MARCH 21 | 12:40AM

INCREDULITY STRUCK ACROSS Bobby Beaker's face as he listened to the three boys weave the story of the treehouse they had secretly built and the body in the woods. As they waited for the police to show up to the house, Mr. Beaker wanted as much information as possible and to find out why these boys were riding their bicycles around the neighborhood at one o'clock in the morning.

"We were in the treehouse when we heard him walking through the woods. We saw him dump the body out there and bury her," Lucas said, his voice trembling at times.

"Yeah," Elijah said. "He buried her and rolled a log on top of the hole."

"Why didn't you tell anyone?" Bobby asked.

All three boys glanced sideways at each other. "We

were afraid of getting in trouble," Lucas said. "We knew we weren't supposed to be out there. And we didn't know what would happen if we went to the police. We thought they'd arrest us."

"We were going to though," Elijah piped up. "But when Lucas and Tyler went back out to the treehouse, it had been destroyed. So then we thought whoever that man was, was watching us, or had at least seen us up there."

"After he chased me in that black car, I knew he was following us," Lucas said.

Police lights lit up the dining room window, the hues of blue and white pulsing through the closed shutters. Mr. Beaker went to the front door to let them in. Tyler's father, John, was with them, still in his street clothes, though he'd put on jeans and a black polo shirt instead of arriving in pajamas.

They entered the house, John with two other officers. He saw his son at the dining room table. He went to his son and grabbed him in a hug. "Are you okay?"

"Yeah, Dad, I'm fine," Tyler said. "But he took Lucas's sister."

Bobby came over to them. "Look at this, John. It's her cellphone. The boys said the guy threw it into a yard across the street. She was talking to some boy named Brandon."

John took the cellphone from Bobby's hand and

read the messages. "The last call on the log was from him. Let's find who this kid is, and let's get a cruiser over to his house immediately," he said to one of the officers with him. Lucas recognized him as the handsome one that had stopped his sister just a few days earlier for running a stop sign.

He turned to the boys, "You saw his car?"

They nodded yes. "A black Ford Five Hundred," Lucas said.

"The same one that chased you the other day?"

Lucas nodded yes.

"Let's get everyone possible on that," John said, turning to the other officer, a Hispanic man not much older than his counterpart. His nametag read OR-TEGA. "And I want a database list of every Ford Five Hundred registered in the county."

Tyler spoke up, sheepishly, "Um, Dad? We already have that." He pulled out the folded paper from his pocket and handed it to John. The man unfolded it, looking at the list, the circled selections.

"Where did you get this?" he asked.

"From your computer," Tyler said apprehensively. "We figured that whoever it was that tried to run over Lucas may have been the same guy that killed Ariana Perez, and we went out to find him. We thought if we could find the same car again, we could tell the cops, and then you could arrest him and search his car for

DNA."

"Did you find him?"

"Yes sir," Tyler said.

"It's the third one circled, Mr. Washington," Elijah said.

"The one on Larkwood," said Lucas. "He has a broken tail light. The passenger side. It's fixed with red tape. We were in his bushes when he left tonight. We followed him back here but didn't make it in time. He took off with Allison, but he threw her phone in the yard over there," Lucas pointed out the window.

"Is this what you boys do at night?" John Washington asked, looking at all three of them. "Play detective?"

They held their heads down in guilt. "I'm sorry, Dad," Tyler said.

"I'm not happy about it, and in fact, it scares me to death," the man said. "But I'll be damned if you ain't the three bravest boys on the planet."

CHAPTER TWENTY SIX
FRIDAY MARCH 21 | 1:13AM

THE MAN IN the glasses led Allison back to the tiny bedroom and motioned for her to sit on the bed. She did so, and he stood in the open doorway. "I don't know when the next you'll get to eat will be," he said. "I am going to make you something."

Something of disgust, subliminal, must have shown across her face because he said, "Don't worry. I'm not going to poison you or anything. Like I told you before, I'm not going to hurt you. I don't want to do this anymore than you want to be here. But this is what we have to do. So, I'm going to make you something to eat. I'm going to lock the door. The windows are bolted shut and there are bars on the outside, so you won't be able to escape. I'll be back in here in twenty minutes."

The door closed behind him and she heard the bolt

click. She breathed a heavy sigh, kicking herself now that she'd left that phone in the bathroom. Had she known she'd be alone now, she'd have more time with it. She just hoped that Lucas would know what to do.

Allison stood up from the bed and checked the window. It was definitely bolted and barred, just as the man had said. It was eerily quiet in here now as she looked around the room. There wasn't much to look at, however. The diminutive bedroom barely held the twin-sized bed on its metal frame. She wondered how many other girls had sat on this same bed, waiting for their fate. Waiting to be picked up and taken to Mexico where they'd be forced to give their bodies to men for money they'd never see.

A chill ran down her spine and she tried to shake the thought from her brain. She looked under the bed to see if there was anything under it, and there was.

Two sets of handcuffs and a chain to link them were coiled underneath, and she felt sad for the girls that were restrained in these, and somewhat selfishly relieved that she was not one of them. She left them coiled in their place and sat back on the mattress.

This man who she was with had been more than polite to her, but something about his demeanor told her that he could be forceful if necessary, though he may not wish to be.

Part of her, however, wanted to take him out herself. She wondered, as she stared at the closed door, if it would be possible to rush the door as he opened it with the food he was preparing for her. She tried to calculate what it would take to catch him off guard and knock him off his feet and make a dash for the front door. Would she be able to create enough force with a running start to do that?

As much as she wanted to, she couldn't bring herself to do it. The fear of failure took over. The man had almost more than told her that Ariana had tried to escape, and she ended up dead in the process. She just hoped that the beacon she'd sent over the phone to her brother would be enough, and that rescue was not far now.

She heard the bolt click in the door before it opened, and the man swung it open. He was carrying a plate with a hamburger on it. He also had a bottle of water. "I had to get you something you can eat with your hands. No utensils. And I hope you like hamburgers." He handed her the plate and the water bottle, which still had the cap snug and seal unbroken.

She took the plate and water from his outstretched hands, looking at the dry hamburger.

"Sorry, there aren't any condiments. But at least it's something," he said.

She didn't know if she could eat at the moment,

with all the nerves and uneasiness coursing through her body. Even looking at the food made her stomach uneasy.

As if he could read her mind, the man said, "I know, it may be hard to force yourself to eat right now, but you have to. I don't know when you'll get your next meal."

As he spoke, he bent down in front of her and caressed her cheek. Allison instinctively pulled away from his touch. "I am truly sorry that I have to do this to you," he said. "I wish there was another way."

Off in the distance, police sirens faintly sung through the night air. He stood up and looked at his watch. "They're out looking for you now," he said. "That didn't take long." He looked back at her. "Please, eat. You'll thank me later for it."

CHAPTER TWENTY SEVEN
FRIDAY MARCH 21 | 12:50AM

"COME ON, TYLER. I'm taking you home," John Washington said to his son. Tyler got up from the dining room table where he, Lucas and Elijah were still sitting. He gave each of his friends a fist bump, not knowing when he'd get to see them again. Despite his dad's words of encouragement, Tyler knew he would probably be grounded for some time.

"Detective Washington," the Hispanic officer approached John. He had just ended a call on his radio. "The boy she was talking with is Brandon Murphy, a Senior at Henderson High. Here's the thing; Officer Sullivan is at the boy's house now. The kid went to a party earlier in the evening, but he's been at home since. Says he hasn't spoken to the girl in days. Looked at his phone, no messages, no outgoing calls to Ms. Beaker."

John Washington was perplexed at this. "He could have easily deleted them from his phone log. Have Sullivan take him to the station for now. We'll question him down there and find out what's going on."

"Yes sir," Officer Ortega said. "But here's the other thing. The Murphys don't live on Larkwood Drive, and they don't own a Ford Five Hundred."

The detective furrowed his eyebrows, deep lines forming in between then.

Stephanie Beaker had appeared from the master bedroom in a pair of blue pajama pants and a sweater. She'd tried to tame her hair in a ponytail, but strands were still sticking out behind her ears. She couldn't believe what she was hearing. "Are you telling me it wasn't this boy? Then who the hell took our daughter?" Her voice had gone from bewilderment to near-anger. Bobby put his arms around his wife to help calm her down.

"I don't know, Stephanie. But I promise you we are going to find her as quickly as possible. Bobby," John said, turning to Lucas's dad, "I'm going to run Tyler home. And then I'm going to check this house out on Larkwood." He held the paper with the addresses. "Ortega will be here if anything changes."

Bobby Beaker let his wife go from his embrace. "Let me go with you, John. That's my daughter out there." John nodded his approval, and the two men, along with Tyler, left. Elijah and Lucas gazed out the window, and watched them, not knowing when they'd get to see their friend again.

"Elijah, we should get ahold of your mother," Stephanie said to her son's friend. "She's going to want you home and safe. What's her phone number?"

Elijah gulped and nervously recited his mother's phone number and Mrs. Beaker called her. She answered, groggy and still half-asleep. "Hi, Crystal, it's Stephanie Beaker, Lucas's mother. Listen, Elijah is over here, and I need you to come get him." A pause. "No, he's not in trouble. We've got a family situation over here, and we think it would be best for him to be with you tonight."

Lucas felt his phone buzz, and he pulled it out of his pocket. He assumed that Tyler would be texting him, but it was a location notification. A new contact, Amilyn Davis, is sharing their location with you the bubble read. He opened up the application, which pulled up a map. He knew that name. Amilyn was his sister's best friend, and she was a common presence in their home, but he'd never talked with her. How did she get his phone number? And why was she sharing her location?

A thought sliced across his mind like a bolt of lightning in a dark sky. He couldn't believe it. It wasn't Amilyn. It was Allison. Why or how she had her friend's phone he didn't know. But staring at the location pinging on his screen, he saw that it was on the south side of town, close to the highway.

Lucas nudged Elijah and showed him the screen. Elijah stared at the device, and then up at Lucas. He mouthed, "What is it?"

Lucas whispered, "Come with me."

As they were staring at the device, Stephanie hung up the phone with Elijah's mom.

"Hey mom," Lucas said, standing up from the table, "Elijah has some stuff in my bedroom that he wants to take back home. I'm going to help him get it."

"Yeah, sure," she said. "Elijah, your mother will be here in about 10 minutes."

"Yes ma'am," Elijah said. He, too, got up from the table and followed Lucas back to his bedroom.

"What is that?" Elijah said, as they shut the bedroom door.

"Bro, this is my sister! She's sending a beacon. I don't know how, but she has her friend's phone. We have to go after her. I need your help."

"We can't go back out there, man! Are you serious? The cops are everywhere!"

"I know, but we have to. This is her call for help, and she sent it to me. Look," he showed Elijah the map again, the location that Allison was sharing was pinging on the screen. "It's less than two miles from here. We can grab the bikes outside and go after her."

"How are we going to rescue her? We don't have any weapons." Elijah said. "Let's just give this to the officer outside and let them handle it."

"No, Elijah." Lucas stood firm. "This is my fault. The man saw us in the treehouse, and he followed us, and he saw her. He's already killed one girl. I'm going after him, whether you come with me or not."

Elijah sighed. "Okay, let's do this. I don't want to see anyone else die."

"Okay, my dad has a nine millimeter in his nightstand. I'm going to get it. We need to get the bikes out of the front yard."

"You're taking a gun?" Elijah said incredulously. "You can't be serious."

"Elijah, it's my sister. Come on, we don't have much time." Lucas pulled his backpack hanging from the closet doorknob. "I'm going to put the gun in here, but I need you to carry it out. We need to leave before your mom gets here."

Lucas opened his bedroom door, making sure his mother couldn't see him. She was now sitting at the dining room table, her head buried in her hands. He wished he could comfort her, but he knew that he and Elijah were on borrowed time. He crossed the hallway to his parents' room and went to the bedside table on Bobby's side of the bed. Opening the top drawer, he saw it. The black handgun in a nylon holster. He took it and felt the weight of the gun in his hands. It was heavier than he thought it would be. Placing it in the main pocket of his backpack, he shut the nightstand drawer and dashed back to his room.

"Ok, I've got it. Let's go." Lucas handed the backpack to Elijah, who swung it over his shoulders.

"Have you ever even shot a gun, Lucas?" Elijah asked.

"Well, no. But how hard can it be? Just point and pull the trigger, right?"

Elijah shrugged his shoulders.

They went to the dining room. "Mom, our bicycles are still in the front yard. Is it okay if we put them in the garage? Elijah said he can come back tomorrow to get his."

Stephanie looked up, her eyes puffy already from crying. "Yes, that's fine."

"Mom, don't worry," Lucas said. He put his arms around her and kissed her on the cheek. "Allison is going to be alright. I promise."

"I certainly hope so, baby," she said and kissed her son on the forehead.

"We'll come back in through the garage door," he said, removing himself from her embrace. Lucas and Elijah went outside to the front yard where the bicycles had been deposited earlier. They could see Officer Ortega in his patrol car, parked out front, his lights still rotating, illuminating the neighborhood. An older couple across the street stood on their front porch, silently watching the way nosey neighbors do.

As the two boys picked up the bicycles from the ground, they gained Ortega's attention. "My mom asked us to take these into the garage," Lucas said, and Ortega nodded. The man went back to concentrating his attention on the computer console in his vehicle.

Lucas and Elijah walked the bicycles to the backside of the house, away from the prying eyes of the neighbors. Lucas pulled out his phone, the beacon still pinging. "We're going to have to go through the alleys. The cops are out looking for her."

The two boys mounted the bicycles, with Lucas riding Tyler's, and they set off to the south end of town. The unpaved alleys were a much rougher ride than the smooth asphalt streets, and Lucas was glad he had Tyler's bike, as the suspension was better than his own for navigating potholes and grooves in the dirt. He also knew he would need the pegs that his own bicycle lacked; once they found Allison, he'd need to get her back home and she'd have to ride standing on them.

"How much further?" Elijah asked.

Lucas looked at the phone. "About four more blocks, and then we need to turn right."

As they came up to their turn, blue lights flashed. "Hide!" Lucas commanded. They jumped behind a large beige dumpster and watched as a police cruiser crept by, its spotlight focused on the alleyways.

"I wonder if they're looking for her, or for us," Elijah pondered.

Lucas's phone dinged with a text message. He opened it. It was from his mom. *Elijah's mother is here. You better get back here now.*

"I think I know the answer," Lucas said, showing the screen to his friend.

Lucas opened up his text messages and swiftly typed out and sent a message to his mom. *I'm sorry mom. We are going to rescue Allison. I love you.*

PART THREE
THE RESCUE

ANDREW J BRANDT

CHAPTER TWENTY EIGHT
FRIDAY MARCH 21 | 1:35AM

THE MAN IN the glasses unlocked the door and came back in to the bedroom. Allison stiffened up, still sitting on the bed where he'd left her.

"They're going to be here any minute. I'm here to collect your trash," he said to her, approaching the bed. He took up the plate, a few crumbs were all that was left of the hamburger he'd fed her. "Good to see you finally ate. And the water?"

She showed him the bottle, an ounce of fluid still in the bottom. "Go ahead and finish that as well. You'll be glad you did tomorrow."

Allison unscrewed the cap, her eyes locked on the man's, and downed the last of the water. She handed him the empty bottle and turned to leave the room.

And just then, something primal inside Allison snapped.

Without even thinking, she rushed the man, his back turned to her, and wrapped her arms around him in a tackle. Through the open door, he hit the wall of the hallway opposite of the bedroom. Her left arm was caught between the man and the wall and she felt the bone in her forearm crack.

The pain made her see stars for a sliver of a second, yet she maintained composure enough to lift her knee in between the man's legs and, with as much force as she could muster, kneed him in the groin.

He yelled profanities and slumped to the floor, grabbing his crotch. Allison clutched her left arm close to her chest and ran down the hallway of the small apartment and frantically searched for a way out.

The hallway spilled out to an open kitchen and living room, both of which were as sparsely decorated as the bedroom she'd been held captive in. There was no couch, no television hanging on the wall, no sign that this place was something lived in. It was a transit station. A place to transfer girls like her—no telling how many had come before—from one person to another. Seller to buyer.

She saw the door, a plain white door with a small rectangular window near the top. She bolted for it and fumbled at the lock on the round silver handle with her one good hand. She quickly realized there were multiple locks to the door, including a sliding chain. Panicking, she slipped the chain, but couldn't get it to release from its saddle.

Her head snapped backward, and she felt several hairs ripped from her scalp. The man was behind her and he pulled her to him and threw her to the ground. Allison kicked and screamed clawed at him as he held her down.

His fist met her eye socket and the back of her head bounced off the vinyl plank flooring from the force. She tried lifting her legs but he was sitting on them, his full weight on top of her.

With her one good arm, Allison reached up and was able to tear the man's glasses from his face and she scraped at the man's eyes with her fingernails. She felt the flesh tear through her fingers and he screamed in agony again.

She tried to wriggle free from his grip but he was too strong. She screamed again, words unintelligible. This guttural, desperate sound pouring from her lungs and throat echoed through the whole apartment.

The man, his face bleeding from her fingernails, headbutted her right on the bridge of her nose and blood immediately gushed from it. Laying on her back, she couldn't breathe and she finally gave up her struggle. The man picked her up from the hair and dragged her back into the bedroom.

201

"I tried being nice to you," he said in a manner too calmly. "I tried to do this the easy way, to show you mercy." His voice was still pleasant and cool, like they were having a conversation during dinner. He tossed her onto the floor of the bedroom and she collapsed in a mess of hair and blood and tears.

"I liked you, Allison," he continued, and he crouched down on the floor in front of her. He ran his hand through her hair and tucked a collection of strands behind her ear. "I made this easy for you because I liked you. Look at me." She looked up at him through her swelling right eye. Her hair fell over her face and was matted with blood from her nose, which still was dripping. He continued, "I wanted this to be easy for you, but you apparently didn't want that. So, when you're in Mexico, being passed from man to man, their sweat and bodies all over you, and there are so many that you can't even feel your womanly parts anymore, just remember that it's your own fault. This is how you wanted it. And remember that it was me who tried to make this easy for you."

He stood up and looked down at her, this bawling mess of a girl. He placed his glasses back on his face. "I've done this too many times to count, Allison. I've had girls who gave in easily and I've had fighters. You're nothing special. Just another paycheck for me."

"You don't even have a family, do you?" she said

through spit and blood. "It was just an act."

The man rolled his eyes. "It does make for a great story, doesn't it? Almost made you feel sorry for me. What can I say? It usually keeps the more aggressive ones a little more docile. A little easier to handle. They think they're helping me out."

"Well," she said, staring at the man with eyes full of rage and despair, "I want you to know that when you're rotting in a jail cell for what you've done, you'll remember me. And you'll know that Allison Beaker was the girl who took you down."

A sound of tires crunching on asphalt outside caught the man's attention. The brakes squeaked and two car doors opened and shut. "That may have to wait," the man said. "Your chariot has arrived."

ANDREW J BRANDT

CHAPTER TWENTY NINE
FRIDAY MARCH 21 | 1:35AM

LUCAS AND ELIJAH approached the place that his phone displayed. It was a nondescript apartment complex of about a dozen buildings. There were four townhouses that lined the path into the complex, and four more buildings on each side of the path behind them. A black electronically-controlled gate blocked the entrance and a large sign, white text on black background, in front of the entrance read "APPLEGATE TOWNHOMES".

His phone buzzed and when he saw the incoming call he gulped. The name on the screen just said "DAD." He answered it. Before his father even had a chance to speak, Lucas said, "Dad, I know you're mad. But just listen."

He couldn't even finish explaining as his father was yelling on the other end of the call, "I don't know what the hell you're thinking but you better get back home right now, son! Your mother is damn near having a panic attack!"

"Dad, listen to me," Lucas said, sternly. "I need you and Tyler's dad to come to the Applegate Townhomes on the southside of town. This is where he took Allison. I'm here now."

"You're what?!"

"I can explain later, Dad. But Allison is here. Elijah and I came to rescue her. So, please, get the cops over here now. I have to go now. I'm sorry." He hung up the phone and put it in his pocket.

Elijah looked at him with a concerned side glance. "You know we're in deep shit, right?"

"Oh yeah." Lucas knew that their parents were losing their minds, but he also knew that he had to come here; that Allison sent him that beacon for a reason.

The two boys walked up to the gate, finding that it was impossible to squeeze through the metal slats. Lucas estimated that it was about ten feet high as well, and there was no real place to grip to climb over. Even if they could reach the top of the gate, coiled barbed wire lined it.

"This place looks like a prison," Elijah said.

"I know. We need to figure out how to get in here though," Lucas said, shaking the bars.

"Does this fence circle the whole complex?" Elijah

asked, examining the gate and fencing.

Lucas walked the length of the fence for a few yards, but as far as he could see, there were no breaks in the slats. Eventually, the metal gating was replaced with a brick wall. It, too, however, was over ten feet tall and had the same barbed wire at the top. "I think so," he conceded

They heard the sound of tires crunching on the loose asphalt and a vehicle turn onto the road leading to the complex. Lucas and Elijah quickly raced their bicycles out of view from the road and they watched as a black Chevy Tahoe approach the gate. The electronic controller to the metal gate engaged, and it was pulled away from the road on a motorized chain. Once the gate opened, the Tahoe drove through.

"Let's go!" Lucas sprinted for the gate and Elijah followed. The gate was closing quickly, and they ran along the perimeter, no more than ten yards between them and the opening.

Lucas jumped through and turned to help Elijah. Elijah put his arm through but pulled it back instinctively as the gate closed between them. "I'm so sorry, Lucas. I tried!" His eyes welled up. "I'm sorry."

"It's okay, Elijah. It'll be okay. Stay by the bikes. My dad and Mr. Washington will be here soon. Keep a look out for them. I'm going for my sister."

"Here," Elijah said, sliding the backpack from his

shoulders. "You're going to need this."

Lucas grabbed the bag and unzipped it, pulling the weapon from its cavity. He held it in his left hand, the muzzle pointed to the ground, and his finger free of the trigger. "Thank you for coming with me. You and Tyler are the best friends I could ever ask for."

Elijah grabbed onto the bars of the gate, like a prisoner peering out from his cell. "Maybe if you find your sister and we can rescue her, our parents will let us hang out again after this."

Lucas smiled and fist bumped Elijah through the gate. He turned to face the apartment complex, knowing that, at least until his dad arrived with Detective Washington, he was completely alone.

The lights from the complex illuminated the driveway, though Lucas followed the path quietly in the shadows. He held the pistol in his hand as he turned a corner.

The black Tahoe was parked in front of one of the townhomes. Lucas watched from behind the corner across the way as two men got out of the car. They were both in business suits. The driver was completely bald on top of his head, with a full beard growing underneath. The other was clean shaven and had long black hair touching his shoulders.

Lucas watched as they stood at the front door. They didn't knock to announce their arrival, they simply stood on the stoop and waited. After about twenty seconds, the door opened.

The man who answered the door, Lucas saw, looked like he'd been in a fist fight. Framed in black wayfarer glasses, his face was dark with blood around his right eye. There was blood on his button-down shirt.

Without a word, the man let the two new arrivals in. Lucas continued to watch. He didn't know what was happening, but he feared the worst. A feeling deep in his gut told him that these men were here to help dispose of a body.

Allison's body.

After a few minutes, the door opened again, and Lucas held his breath. The man in the glasses came out first, and then the two men in suits.

Along with Allison.

Lucas could see her. He could tell that she was injured and bleeding, but she was alive. She was holding her right arm close to her body. Her head was held down low in defeat. She walked slowly, dragging her feet while the two suits led her to the Tahoe. The man in glasses opened the back passenger door for them.

He couldn't believe it. The feeling of elation, however, quickly turned to rage. He realized that his sister was injured because of the man in glasses. She had apparently tried to fight him, to escape, and by the looks of it, she lost. He wondered if that was how the other girl, the one buried in the woods, had lost her life. If she, too, tried to escape and this man killed her for it.

From his lookout point and filled with rage and despair, Lucas raised the gun in his hand, aimed it at the man in glasses and pulled the trigger.

CHAPTER THIRTY
FRIDAY MARCH 21 | 1:40AM

ELIJAH HEARD ANOTHER car approach the complex behind him and he moved away from the gate. Just as he and Lucas did earlier, he hid in the grass off to the side of the entrance of the apartment complex and watched as the new arrival pulled up, the headlights of the vehicle off and dark.

Two men got out of the car, an unmarked police cruiser in a charcoal gray, and a tall black man emerging from the driver's side. Elijah immediately recognized them. He jumped up from his prone position in the grass. "Mr. Washington!" he called out and ran toward them.

John Washington turned to see the boy running toward him. "Elijah?" he asked. As the boy got closer, John Washington could see that it was, indeed, Tyler's friend Elijah. "What is going on here, son?" he asked.

"We think this is where he took Allison," Elijah said.

Bobby Beaker exited from the passenger side of the vehicle. "Elijah, where is Lucas?" he asked sternly.

Elijah pointed to the gate. "He went in. A black SUV came up to the gate and he got through before it closed again."

John went to the keypad near the gate. The metal box was mounted on a steel pole about four feet high.

"Do you know the code to get in?" Bobby asked.

"All of these complexes and gated communities have emergency codes programmed in for EMS and police. I'm trying to remember it. It's been a while since I was on patrol," he said as he thumbed at the control box. He pressed a few buttons and the panel beeped, but the gate did not open. He repeated this effort a few times, cursing every time it didn't work.

Bobby turned back to Elijah. "You said a black SUV came in here? Did you see the black car?"

"Right," Elijah said. "An SUV, a Tahoe I think, pulled in about ten minutes ago. We didn't see the car that took Allison. But we know this is where he brought her. She's definitely in there."

"How do you know that?"

"Because she shared her location with Lucas earlier. Like, on his phone. He could see it on the map."

John looked up from the keypad and at Bobby, both men perplexed. "What do you mean? Her phone was tossed in a yard across the street from our house. We have her phone." Bobby said.

"Right. But she somehow had her friend's phone, and she sent Lucas the location. So, we rode over here to rescue her."

Suddenly, Bobby remembered. Allison's friend Amilyn had been over earlier in the evening, but she'd left well before Allison was taken. What he didn't understand was why did Allison have Amilyn's phone?

As they were talking, the gate rumbled to life and the motorized chain began to pull it open. "Got it!" John Washington said and pumped his fist.

"Elijah, I need you to stay here in the car. Lock the doors," John said. "Bobby, in the center console is a Walther. Get it." The detective pulled his own weapon, a Glock 22, from his hip holster.

Lucas opened the back door of the cruiser and sat in the backseat. It was plastic and uncomfortable. A metal barrier separated him from the front seats. He'd never been in the back of a cop car before, and despite it not being very comfortable, he felt safe in here instead of hiding in the grass out in the open.

As the two men entered the gate on foot, a blast rang through the air. They both quickly realized it was the sound of a gunshot. The two men looked at each other and sprinted as fast as they could toward the interior of the complex.

CHAPTER THIRTY ONE
FRIDAY MARCH 21 | 1:44AM

THE MAN IN the glasses, standing by the open Tahoe door, dropped to the ground, writhing and screaming in pain. The bullet hit him below the knee, tearing through the flesh and bone in his shin. Several expletives left his mouth as he held on to his leg.

Lucas opened his eyes and peered around the corner of his hiding spot to see the chaos and commotion his gunshot created. He couldn't hear anything but a high-pitched ringing, the blast was louder than he'd thought it would be. The two men escorting Allison to the car surveyed their surroundings frantically, searching for the source of the shot that hit the man with the glasses.

Lucas stayed hidden behind the corner of the building, hoping they could not see him and hoping that his distraction would help Allison escape. However, the men had a firm grasp on her and led her to the vehicle. She was crying frantically now, struggling in the arms of her new captors.

As they forced her into the backseat of the Tahoe, another shot rang through the night air and dust puffed up from the ground around the men's feet, nearly hitting the man in glasses again. However, this one wasn't from Lucas, and he searched for the source. He saw them, coming toward the Tahoe.

He instantly recognized them, under the moonlight. His dad and John Washington ran up on the scene, weapons drawn. "Police! Get on the ground!" Detective Washington yelled. He repeated the command, and the two men in suits dropped to their knees, with their hands above their heads.

John and Bobby approached slowly now, their weapons raised and readied on the men. John reached for a radio clipped to his belt.

"Dispatch, this is Detective Washington. We've got a 10-71 at the Applegate Townhomes. Location, 10121 South Pheasant Drive. I repeat, 10-71, requesting backup. Suspects in custody."

A woman's voice crackled through the other end and confirmed his request. Almost immediately, sirens could be heard in the distance.

As they approached, Bobby could see Allison's legs sticking out from the backseat of the Tahoe. "Allison?"

he called out.

"I'm here, Bobby!" she said through her tears.

John Washington stepped behind the men and grabbed one of them by the arms. He twisted the man's hands behind his back and secured them with a pair of handcuffs and then pressed the man to the ground. "Bobby," he said, "get this one."

Bobby came around slowly, weapon stayed on the man still on his knees. John reached down into his pocket and pulled out a bundle of thick zip ties. "This will have to do for now," he said. Bobby took them and tied the second suited man's hands behind his back. He pressed the man to the ground as John Washington turned his attention to the man in glasses.

"You got the raw end of this deal tonight, didn't you?" John said to the man as he examined the gunshot wound. "We're gonna get you fixed up so you don't bleed out on us. But your night isn't over." John zip tied the man's hands in front of this body and helped the man lean against the front tire of the Tahoe.

John reached for his radio again. "Dispatch, Detective Washington. 10-52 here at the Applegate. We've got one wounded."

"10-4, Detective."

Bobby finally took his attention away from the bounded men and went to the open passenger door of the Tahoe. He saw Allison there, sobbing and covered in dirt and blood. She held her broken arm against her chest. "Allison," he said, tears welling up in his eyes. "Oh my god, baby girl, are you okay?"

"Yeah, I am now. I was so scared," she said. "And arm is broken."

"Let's get you out of here," he said, as he lifted her out of the Tahoe.

Three police cruisers drove up to the scene, lighting up the entire parking lot. Officer Ortega and Officer Sullivan came up to John Washington to await their orders. "Get these men in a cruiser," the detective said.

The officers grabbed the men in suits and Officer Sullivan replaced the zip ties on the one with long hair with metal handcuffs. The two officers then roughly led them to their vehicles, depositing the bounded men in the backseats.

Once they were secured, Officer Sullivan shut the door to the cruiser and approached Detective Washington again. "Sir," he said. "I've run into this young woman a couple of times. With your permission, I'd like to escort her and her father to the hospital."

"Thank you, officer," John said.

As Officer Sullivan walked Bobby and Allison to his cruiser, Lucas appeared from his hiding spot. "Dad!" he yelled out. Bobby turned to see his son behind the corner of the building.

"Lucas!" he shouted.

Lucas ran up to his father and wrapped his arms around the man. "Dad, you rescued us!"

"I am so glad you're safe, son. You don't know how scared I was tonight."

"Dad, I took your gun. I'm sorry."

Bobby's eyes widened. "You did what? Where is it now?"

"I left it behind the building over there." Lucas released himself from his father's grip. "I shot him. I didn't know what to do. They were going to take her, and I had to do something. So, I shot him."

"Officer Sullivan," Bobby said, turning to the officer escorting them. "Will you retrieve the Glock that Lucas left behind that building?"

Sullivan nodded and did so. Bobby turned back to his son. "I don't know what to say, son. I'm mad and scared and just happy that you're safe. That both of you are."

They continued to Officer Sullivan's police cruiser and got in. Sullivan hopped in the driver's seat.

"Sullivan," Bobby said, "there's another boy in John's car. We need to get him as well."

Allison leaned against Bobby. "You're my hero, Dad."

* * *

The hospital was cold, as hospitals usually are, and Lucas sat in a plastic chair next to Allison's bed. His eyes were heavy as he looked at his sister, now in a hospital gown and cleaned up from the altercation. Her arm had been set and was in a cast and she slept soundlessly, knocked out from a mix of pain medication and exhaustion.

Bobby and Stephanie leaned over their daughter, watching her sleep. A knock at the door startled them, and they all turned to see John Washington at the doorway.

"How is she doing?" he asked.

"Sleeping like a baby," Stephanie said.

"We got some information for you guys, I thought you'd like to know as soon as possible," the detective said.

He had a folder tucked under his arm and he opened it up. Pulling out a sheet from the folder, he handed it to Bobby. "His name is Adam Reese. Thirty-seven years old. He admitted to the murder of Ariel Perez, but claims it was an accident. After he's sentenced, he'll be behind bars for the rest of his life."

The Beakers looked at the paper and read over the charges. Adam Reese's mugshot, taken shortly after his arrest earlier in the night, was in the top right corner of the page. The man had no previous convictions, no previous arrests.

"What about the guys he was working with?" Stephanie asked.

"Two Mexican nationals. Brothers. Will be charged with kidnapping and human trafficking. Their M.O. fits with several other kidnappings throughout east and south Texas. They'll probably be extradited, but the Texas Rangers are working on finding the eight other girls we think they're responsible for taking."

John turned his attention to Lucas. "You boys did a dangerous thing tonight. But also, very brave. I don't know how your parents feel right now, but I want you to know that the entire police force is grateful for what you, Tyler and Elijah did tonight."

Lucas looked at his parents. "I'm sorry that I scared you guys. I just wanted to save my sister. I kind of forced Elijah to come with me so I hope he's not in too much trouble."

Bobby said, "I know, son. Like Mr. Washington says, it was very dangerous. You could have been seriously hurt or killed. But it's all over now, and you're all safe."

Lucas leaned back into his chair and shut his eyes. No longer able to hold it back, he fell into a deep, dreamless sleep.

ANDREW J BRANDT

EPILOGUE
SATURDAY JUNE 14 | 9:20PM

INSTEAD OF BEING built around a tree, the base was made from four nine-foot four-by-four planks, screwed together in a square. From there, four more four-by-fours were erected to make the legs, to which the floor was attached. With two-by-four planks set parallel creating some support, two sheets of plywood were screwed down atop these to create a floor, and the walls were covered in plywood. A rope ladder hung from the entrance cut into one side, and the roof was covered by a blue tarp, stapled down to the support beams.

The new fort looked over the brown wooden fence that ringed the Beakers' backyard. From a window cut into the wall facing the east, they could see the edge of the woods. With the help of Bobby and John, the three boys were able to salvage some of the materials from their old treehouse in the forest and, with the blessing of their parents, built the new fort here.

The sound of cicadas echoed through the warm summer air. Even after sunset, the temperature was still hovering around eighty degrees. A breeze flowing in from the Gulf of Mexico made it bearable, however, and the temperature would continue to drop to more comfortable levels.

Inside the fort, Lucas, Tyler and Elijah were sorting out their items, laying down sleeping bags and pillows. Tyler pulled out a Bluetooth speaker and turned it on. He cycled through some music on his phone until he found a song he wanted. Post Malone started playing through the little speaker and he sat it in the corner.

When she came home from her new summer job at the pizzeria on Kilgore Drive, Allison had brought the boys a pizza. "Consider it a housewarming gift," she said. Now Elijah had two slices stacked on top of each other, cramming as much as he could into his mouth.

Lucas held a nail between his thumb and forefinger and hammered gently to get it started into the wood. He continued pounding until he had the page nailed down in all four corners. Once finished, he stepped back to admire his work.

The poster, their first piece of decoration, was the

laminated front page of a recent issue of the Henderson News. The cover story above the fold read LOCAL BOYS HELP RESCUE GIRL, SOLVE MURDER CASE.

"Definitely better than the Avengers," Elijah said, his mouth full of pizza.

Tyler nodded in agreement. "I've never seen Iron Man on the front page of the paper."

As the music continued playing, Lucas smiled, admiring the poster. With his two best friends, he was ready to have the best summer ever and spend every night possible right here, in their fort.

ANDREW J BRANDT

ALSO BY ANDREW J BRANDT

THE ABDUCTION OF SARAH PHILLIPS

IN THE FOG

PALO DURO: A THRILLER

AMERICAN ATONEMENT (NOV 2020)

ANDREW J BRANDT

ABOUT THE AUTHOR

Andrew J Brandt is the #1 Amazon bestselling author of multiple novels, including the #1 young adult thriller *The Treehouse*. His works have been international hits. He resides in Texas with his wife and children.

For more information on new releases and author events, find Andrew online at:

www.writerbrandt.com

Made in the USA
Monee, IL
03 April 2020